THE SIEGE AT RHYKER'S STATION

Also by Lee Martin

The Darringer Brothers Series:

THE SIEGE
AT RHYKER'S
STATION

LEE MARTIN

Vaca Mountain Press
Vacaville, California, USA

Vaca Mountain Press
Paperback ISBN 13: 978-1-952380-55-6
Kindle ISBN 13: 978-1-952380-56-3

Also available in:
Large Print Paperback ISBN 13: 978-1-952380-61-7

Cover design by Christopher and Deirdre Wait,
High Pines Creative, for ENC Graphic Services
Cover photographs © Getty Images

Published by Vaca Mountain Press
Vacaville, California, U.S.A.

Visit Lee Martin Westerns on Facebook.

To my wonderful family
and in memory of
my dear sister and best friend Arlene,
and of our loving mother,
our rough riding brothers,
and of Jim Liontas

THE SIEGE
AT RHYKER'S
STATION

CHAPTER 1

In West Texas during the War Between the States in 1864, night riders in dark clothes attacked a shirt tail spread in bright moonlight. With torches, they set fire to the house and barn, but did free the horses. Firing wildly in the night, they came to terrorize and murder. Flames shot in crimson and yellow toward the sky. White smoke billowed as ashes flew in the wind.

Leaving the porch, the badly wounded rancher, unarmed and wearing his nightshirt, crawled on his hands and knees, trying to reach the men dragging his wife toward a shed. One had his grip on her long yellow hair. One of the raiders shot him in the back, leaving him to fall face down as her screams rang out loud and shrill.

A barefoot ten-year-old boy, wearing a blue nightshirt and carrying a heavy shotgun, came running out of the house, stumbled past his father and kept going. Before he could get to his mother, he was hit from behind with the butt of a rifle. He fired both barrels and two men ahead of him jerked and fell.

The boy crumbled face down, unconscious. One of the men picked him up by the seat of his britches and hauled him over to an abandoned, hand dug well.

The boy came to and swung his fists wildly in mid air as he

was carried. His mother's screams from the shed were suddenly silenced. Horses ran wild in terror of the raging red fires. Smoke continued to rise, white and gray against the moon. Ashes flew higher and higher.

At the dry well, the rope wound tight around the windlass was old and rotting.

On the crumbling adobe brick rim of the square opening, the boy grabbed the rope high above the now dangling oak bucket. He held on, even as the man threw him bodily off the rim. As the boy clung to the wiry rope, unable to climb up, the big man laughed like a fiend and freed the handle on the windlass.

"Have a good time," the man snickered.

The clogged rope struggled to unwind, even with the boy's weight as he dangled a few feet down into a sixty foot deep, six by six foot square hole. Abruptly, the rope freed itself. The iron handle spun fast and caught the raider's left hand with a loud snap, breaking bone as the man cussed and howled in pain.

The boy dropped with wild swings as he clung to the rope for dear life, trying to get his foot into the wooden bucket. A silent scream caught in his throat as he hurtled downward into the black depths. All of a sudden, the rope jammed again on the windlass, jerking him to a wild halt some twenty feet from the damp, earthen bottom. Badly hurt, he held on to the bucket as he swung in a circle, then jerked back around.

High above, the furious man with the broken left wrist and fingers yelled down into the black hollow. "I shoulda just shot you, you little creep!"

The brute drew his hunting knife with his free right hand and cut the rope at the edge of the windlass. It frayed, then began to unfurl again.

Dropping again, clinging to the rope, the boy prayed for help. He was ten feet from the bottom of the dark pit.

Again the big man slashed at the rope in another spot.

Now the rope began to unfurl again, then jammed. This time the knife cut through the heavy strands.

Down the boy went, tumbling with the bucket and crashing at the bottom. In great pain, he rolled to a stop. The rest of the oily rope came crashing down on the boy and heaped around him.

Above, the big man drew his revolver and leaned over to fire into the well, but his load was empty. He holstered and turned away in agony. His cussing could be heard as he walked away.

Below in the well, with the last of his mother's screams still shattering him, his body wracked in pain from the fall, the boy stared up at the starry sky which looked far, far away in the square frame. He prayed for help. He tried to move. He fought to erase his mother's screams. He could smell the smoke. In his misery, he slowly lost consciousness.

Early the next morning, deep in the well on damp ground, the boy awakened to see the sunlight beaming far above. The bucket and heap of the cut rope were still clustered around him.

He heard a commotion, hoof beats, shouts, then silence. He rose up and yelled until he was hoarse. Then abruptly, he saw the figure of a youth at the rim looking down who suddenly yelled to him.

"Hold on! We'll get some ropes together!"

The boy sat back down and waited. He was in great pain. Finally, a tightly knotted string of ropes came hurtling down. The end rope had a huge noose fastened securely. He heard a man shout from above.

"Get your foot in the loop and hang on."

The boy obeyed, despite his pain, and held on to the rope as best he could as he was pulled to safety.

As the youth and several men helped him from the rim to the

ground, the boy cried out in agony. He hurt from his feet, up his legs, around his back, through his hands and arms, and had a wretched headache. They wrapped a blanket around him, but he could not stop shivering.

"We don't know who done it," the youth said.

Lifted by one of the men, the boy burst into tears when he saw the house, the sheds and buildings all in a heap of ashes and hot embers. He buried his face in the man's heavy shirt. He felt himself hugged, now, so tight it should have hurt, but instead it gave him comfort.

The lone survivor, the boy vowed silently to never let it rest.

*　　*　　*　　*　　*

In fall of 1878 in the wonderlands of New Mexico Territory with its red earth, soft yellow cliffs, green yucca, and scattered silver sage, trouble was ever brewing. From the spread wings of the turkey buzzard to the slinking glass-eyed coyote, life stirred in the prairie, for good or bad.

In the dusty little town of Three Wells, it was a lazy Sunday just at daybreak. County Sheriff Hank Miller stood in the open doorway of his office. Middle-aged with a gray handlebar mustache, he gazed up the near-empty, dusty street. Beyond rose soft yellow bluffs with crimson streaks. There was no wind.

A dedicated but weary lawman, he thought more and more of retiring.

Slowly, he turned to where his elderly jailer, Old Tom, was shaking the coffee pot on the iron stove. Way back in the jail cells, the loud snoring of two drunks could be heard.

Sheriff Miller pushed his hat back as he turned out the lamp burning on the wall hook, then sat down behind his cluttered desk. "Did my daughter make that coffee last night?"

"Yeah, but it was too weak, so I added some grounds."

Tom served them both coffee and sat in front of the desk.

"I wish she'd go visit her aunt," the sheriff said. "Get her away from that Jody Callahan."

"He's sure been courting her. And scaring off the competition, I'm willing to bet. The Callahans own half this territory and aren't bashful about it."

"Teaching school may be proper but that's no life for her either."

All of a sudden at the open door stood Trixie, a saloon woman with a long duster over her scanty, violet-laced garb. Bushy blonde hair in disarray, heavy with the scent of sweet perfume, she was frantic, her voice shrill but low.

"Sheriff, Jody Callahan is drunk over at the saloon. He knocked Posey down the stairs, and she's plumb dead. The barkeep went looking for his pa and brother on account of they was staying at the hotel last night."

"Posey?" Tom murmured. "She was the sweet one."

Sheriff Miller hurried to his feet, strapped on his gun belt and grabbed a loaded shotgun. "You stay here," he said to her, and to Tom, "Look after her."

Tom motioned to Trixie to come over and sit as he poured her coffee. They watched the sheriff leave. Tom shook his head, always worried about the lawman.

"It was so bad," Trixie whispered, cup in both hands. "Jody knocked Posey off the stairs, and he walked right past her body, like he didn't see her lying there. Then he was waving his pistol around like he was going to shoot up the place."

"Did he?" Tom asked.

"He was too drunk." She sipped her coffee. "And nobody could do anything about it, because he's Blair Callahan's baby boy."

"So Blair and the kid's brother are at the hotel?"

"That's what I heard."

Tom suddenly got to his feet and grabbed a shotgun. He checked the load and headed for the front door, knowing it was unlikely he could catch up with the sheriff before he got to the saloon.

While Sheriff Miller came down the street, a heavily intoxicated Jody Callahan stumbled around the empty saloon. Cards were strewn on the tables, along with half empty beer glasses, all left by the hurried departure of nervous customers.

Tilly, a saloon worker, wearing carrot red silk the color of her hair, stood at the top of the stairs just a few feet from a door she could run into and lock behind her. Fearful, she gripped the landing rail for a long moment to gaze at the trouble below, then backed away.

"God help us," she whispered aloud.

Jody Callahan, staggering and stupidly drunk, wandered around the empty tables. Good looking in rumpled but fine clothing, he had dark hair that lay flat and damp. Unkempt but clean-shaven, he finally sat at a table with a bottle of whiskey in front of him. He put his head down as he knocked his glass aside and seemed to be passed out, until he jerked upright and stared into space.

The barkeep entered from the swinging doors and stopped. He looked at Jody and shook his head. Everyone was afraid to criticize a Callahan, especially Jody, his father's pride and joy. Having asked the hotel clerk to tell Blair Callahan about the trouble, the barkeep felt he had done enough. He made his way to the back storeroom and stayed there.

The body of Posey, a saloon worker, had been dragged out of sight.

Jody had no idea she had died. He only knew he was getting sick to his stomach. He could always count on his father and brother to collect him on their way back to the ranch. He just wasn't sure he could wait any longer. He was about to wet his britches.

6

*   *

Outside in the dusty street and headed for the saloon, Sheriff Miller walked alone with his shotgun. No one was visible along the boardwalk. The alleys seemed to be empty and silent.

He was tired of the trouble the Callahans always seemed to make in town. Jody, at times, acted like a silly kid. Blair Callahan, on the other hand, always acted like he was king of the territory.

Sid, Blair's oldest son, fancied himself the fastest draw west of the Mississippi and often buffaloed others into backing off—but Sid had notches on his gun, real and for show.

Yet as the weary sheriff closed in on the saloon where three horses stood at the rail, two rapid shots rang out behind him from a nearby alley. He was hit twice in the back, causing him to stagger then come to a halt. He tried to draw his Colt but went numb.

Sheriff Miller, dead on his feet, jerked and hit the ground.

Coming down the street, Tom stopped in his tracks and lowered his shotgun. He stood in horror as tears filled his eyes.

*   *   *   *   *

On a Saturday night in spring of 1879, far out and to the west in the rangeland of New Mexico Territory, the Callahan Ranch house—grand and stately with two levels—was alive with a wedding reception just inside the main entrance on the first floor.

In front of the colorful garden, buggies and saddle horses were lined up at a rail just short of the picket fence. Music and loud laughter from inside the house rocked the large porch which circled the front and sides of the building. Lights from the front windows flickered, while moonlight came and went with the moving clouds.

Coming out alone on the side porch, to the left of the entrance and facing the vast garden, Jocelyn Miller Callahan, a bride at the age of twenty-two, looked lost and bewildered. With lots of golden hair flowing to her shoulders and down her back, she had an incredibly beautiful face with eyes the dark blue of a mountain lake at sunset. Wearing a soft white, lace-trimmed wedding gown with flowing skirts and veil, she did not look happy or at peace.

With a dark chilly night and only occasional moonlight, she could hide in the shadows. She gave all the appearance of a bride who was really sorry she took the step. A bride who looked ready to run away.

Yes, she had been alone after her father was shot down in the street. And yes, she had an aunt back East—a snobbish woman who had no interest in her—but Jocelyn had no one else. Teaching school had left her drained. Marriage was to be an escape from grief and loneliness to finally say yes to Jody Callahan. No other men had dared to court her.

So she had, just an hour ago, said yes in front of the preacher. Her father had not been there to walk her down the aisle. He had been her comfort, her joy, the only one in her life to have counseled her, and had considered himself her protector. With no mother, she had looked to him for guidance most of her life. And he was gone.

Now she was here with rings on her left hand, all alone with a new set of in-laws who seemed brutal, insensitive, and overbearing. The women in the house were just visitors with lots of food, punch, and a wedding cake. They had been very careful about being too friendly with the bride.

Jocelyn had felt on display when dancing with Jody. As much as he adored her and said he wanted to make her happy, she still wanted to run away, but to what and where? She felt lost forever.

She moved from the side steps into the garden where tall vines had roses in bloom with a sweet scent. She gathered her skirts and trailing veil as she walked on the stone path in soft white shoes, further and further from the music. Like a trapped animal, she stared into the distance.

Lord, she thought, *if there's a way out, please help me find it.*

She heard voices on the porch and now approaching the garden. She backed away behind the tallest rose bushes with their yellow blooms. She sat on a bench, unseen. She hunched down.

Through the bushes, she saw her new brother-in-law, forty-year-old Sid Callahan. With pale blue eyes, Sid sported a dark, trim mustache. Well-dressed, he was as good looking as his brother Jody, the groom. Sid swaggered like a man with whom no one dared trifle. Jocelyn was afraid of him. His kiss for the bride had been unwelcome.

Joining him at the edge of the garden was his sixty-three-year-old father. Blair Callahan had piercing blue eyes and gray hair with a thin mustache and white beard. He had a game right leg. Even in his Sunday-go-meeting suit, Blair looked like the man he was, a tyrant who took no nonsense from anyone. Surly, easily combative, he ruled his family, his ranch, and half of the territory. He gave no quarter. He had not even stooped to kissing his son's bride, as if it had to be the other way around or not at all.

Father and son stood near the garden, unaware Jocelyn sat in hiding and within earshot. She shivered, afraid of giving herself away, and hunched down all the more.

Blair took a bite of chewing tobacco, then pocketed it. "Sure is noisy in there."

Sid nodded. "Big night for Jody."

"Maybe she'll keep him out of trouble."

"Good thing she doesn't know we got rid of her pa," Sid remarked.

Blair pushed his hat back. "No way he was going to hang my son for killing some floozy."

Unseen by the men, Jocelyn covered her mouth to stop an

outcry. She was shaking down to her soft shoes. Tears blurred her vision.

Towering over his father, Sid stretched, rubbed his eyes. "Posey was no loss. Neither was the sheriff. But you know, I could have taken him face on. He never saw the day he could out-draw Sid Callahan."

"Sure enough, but then Jody wouldn't have his bride, because no way she would have married him if she knew all of it. But no more of this. Let it be."

"Yeah, okay." Sid never missed a chance to brag about his skills to his father, and yet he knew Blair still always favored Jody. *Yeah, Pa*, he thought to himself, *you feel guilty because you knew Ma was poorly, but you wanted another son, and she died having him. So here I am, the best you got, and you baby that kid because he's soft like she was. And as long as you have him, she's still alive. Well, so be it. But I'm the fastest gun you ever had. And I can say this—no bride would have run away from me, and that's a fact.*

Behind the tall roses, a horrified Jocelyn hid on the bench, covering her mouth with her hands, silencing her screams as tears ran down her face. Learning why her father had been shot in the back, and that Sid had killed him, terrified her. What's worse, Jody had killed a woman? That came as a shock to her, because Jody had always seemed more gentle than the other Callahans.

Heart racing, face suddenly damp, she trembled with the dread of being seen.

The two men remained within earshot as Sid grumbled aloud. "You've been looking after that kid since he was born. He's spoiled rotten. But now he's got a real decent woman, he won't know what to do with her, right, Pa? Maybe I should give him some pointers."

Blair spat tobacco juice, just missed Sid.

"Hey, watch out, will you?"

Blair just snickered.

The two men turned and moved back toward the front porch.

Jocelyn stayed in the dark, behind the roses. Shaken, terrified, feeling very alone, she knew she had to escape somehow. Wracked with fear, she peered through the vines.

Loud music and laughter continued to roar from inside.

Coming out the front door and closing it behind him, Jody Callahan joined his father and brother as they returned to step up on the porch, standing in the light coming from the windows and the passing moonlight.

Jody, who'd just turned thirty, was clean-shaven and boyishly handsome, well-dressed, and intoxicated. Like his brother, he had dark hair and pale blue eyes. He swayed with a glass in hand. He looked joyful but wimpy.

Sid grabbed Jody's shoulder to steady him. Jocelyn could just hear them.

Jody whined. "Can't find my bride."

Sid burst out laughing. "Maybe she's hiding."

"What?"

Sid finally stopped laughing. "Come on, kid. We'll get you some coffee."

Blair nodded. "Son, she's just getting prettied up for you."

"Yeah," Sid told Jody. "Just ask your Uncle Pike. He had three wives."

Sid and Blair, still amused, hustled Jody back inside to the noise and music. The door closed after them. Figures could be seen through the curtains, but no one else was outside.

Behind the roses on the bench, Jocelyn, horrified at what she'd heard, got to her feet. Faced with going back inside to change clothes for her escape and being stopped, she did the only thing she could. She unhooked the veil from the jeweled clips on her crown of flaxen hair. She rolled it up and shoved it in the bushes. *Lord*, she thought, *please, I need your help.*

She moved quickly, circling through the garden, hunched down away from the window light, reaching the garden gate. Hurrying, she ignored the buggies and chose a quiet, bay saddle horse with a canteen dangling from the horn. A possible sack was tied down with the bedroll behind the cantle.

She paused to tighten the cinch and drop the stirrup. It turned its head to look back at her but didn't shy away.

Taking the reins, she whispered a prayer, *Dear God, please!*

She swung up into the saddle with great difficulty because the stirrups were too long for her. Legs dangling, she rode into the night with skirts draped around her and the now nervous animal. Knowing there were night riders at the herd to the west, and guards on the road to the east and the distant town, she tried to work her way north with the cover of clouds often obscuring the moon and stars.

She knew that in town, there would be no safety from the Callahans. She had a thought to reach the mountains to the north and keep riding through them until she could drop east to find the stage road and beg for a ride.

During the night, she crossed the grassland, sometimes scattering unseen varmints, and climbed the terrain. She circled tall yucca with its clustered, creamy white flowers and busy moths. She struggled through heavy brush with the musky scent of creosote. She then rode high into the mountains where dark, clumped junipers and eerie, rocky terrain kept forcing her to change direction. Ever present were spatters of colorful dirt along the trails, like the rising cliffs that changed color in the moonlight.

She knew she could only move under whatever cover was available by day. The ridges above, however, would give a view of her path. She might be spotted from the high trails.

*　*　*　*　*

Back at the Callahan Ranch late that night, the reception crowd began to leave. Many of the merchants, ranchers and hands were intoxicated. Their well-dressed ladies worried about a safe trip home. None had been invited to stay the night. Nor had the preacher.

The three Callahans said goodbye from the porch.

Late to the reception and now joining them on the porch was sixty-seven-year-old Pike Callahan, Blair's older brother and a good-sized grumpy fellow. Clean-shaven with receding hair, Pike had a twisted left hand he often hid from view, and which he made up for by being a fast draw with his right.

They watched as many of the visitors began to disappear into the night.

Some of the cowhands were finishing a bottle before mounting their horses. They laughed and joked outside of the garden before riding away. Moonlight, often obscured by clouds, showed them the way home.

With only the Callahans returning inside the house to the messy front room, Jody, tipsy, with his jacket off, came out of the back bedroom where his bride should have been waiting. He looked perplexed, torn with anger and distress. Weaving, unstable, he wiped his brow with the back of his hand.

"Where is she?" Jody whined as he plopped down in a chair.

Sid shook his head but took a look outside on the porch and garden. He paused to watch the laughing men who were standing by their horses, not yet ready to leave, still clustered outside the gate.

Blair checked other rooms. Sid returned inside. Pike, plumped down on a sofa, tried not to grin. Jody sat in his chair, dazed, his face pink.

The Callahans paused to assess the situation. Lamplight flickered, casting shadows.

Just then the front door swung open. A disgruntled aging cowhand, beard wet with whiskey, came back inside. He looked frustrated. "My horse is gone."

Jody, wide-eyed, half rose.

"Take one from the corral," Blair said. "Tell the foreman I said to write you a bill of sale, no charge."

The cowhand saluted and staggered back outside, closing the door behind him.

"Who was that?" Pike asked.

"Saddle tramp. Riding the grub line," Blair answered. "We offered him a job, but he wanted to move on. He's headed south."

Jody sank with his face in his hands. He shook with a sob. His wedding had been more than for love of a girl. It had been also to prove to his father that he was a man, maybe not as tough as Sid, but worthy.

Sid had no idea of Jody's motives. "Don't you worry, kid. We'll find her."

Pike folded his arms and rested easy on the sofa. "My second wife ran away like the first, but I just let her go. There's always another one when you know where to look."

"What about the third?" Sid asked.

"Yeah, she emptied my pockets and took off while I was sleeping."

Blair grunted, wanting to tell his brother to shut up, but at the same time, envying Pike because, all the while, Blair was working hard to make their late father's ranch bigger and bigger, pulling strings and running roughshod over anyone in the way, and Pike was out having the time of his life.

*　*　*　*　*

As days passed, Jocelyn hid in the rugged mountains, sustained with the food and blankets she found on the saddle. She knew to stay out of sight as much as possible, keeping to arroyos and narrow passages, and where the trees were more frequent.

She fought off creepy crawlies, avoided snake hideouts, watched a turkey buzzard on the prowl in the sky, went out of her way to avoid a skunk, and was bitten by flying insects. She hurt all over, was often too hungry as she tried to stretch her food, and let her tears flow many times a day.

Deep in the mountains in hazy sun one morning, she heard chattering wrens and saw chipmunks, striped from head to tip of tail, darting around for a look at her. They were welcome company. Not so the lizards which often snuck around her. Cold camping at night and riding north by day, she had chills and fever. Her strength was ebbing.

With little water and poor forage in the rocky crimson and gold terrain, the bay tried many times to fight the bit and head for home. Growing weaker by the day, she knew her chances for survival were slim.

She had often used a blanket to sweep away her horse's tracks but now it was too rocky to worry. At night, she would pray over and over, "Lord, thank you for the warning and for getting me here. Please give me strength to go on. Please help me get away."

Nights, the coyotes barked and howled from far away. She wanted to talk back to them, to anyone. Lonely and desperate, her only solace was that she was not lying in Jody's arms, knowing what she had learned.

At an early dawn many days later, shivering in her tattered dress as she tried to tighten the cinch, the already barn-sour bay pinned its ears back, jerked around, and kicked over some rocks while knocking her aside. She fell back and landed hard.

The loud rattle from an annoyed diamondback startled the bay, which reared and spun, taking her blankets and food with it as it headed for home. She got up, stumbled back from the sound of the rattler and fell again on the rocky ground. The bay disappeared through the trees and rocks, leaving only the echo of its hooves.

"Dear God," she sobbed, hugging herself.

Frantic, knowing her mount could be tracked back to her, she was all the more careful from then on to keep out of sight from the ridges above to the west. She began a painful hike north through brush that tore her dress, and over rocks that caused her to fall again. Her soft shoes wore thin and her feet became sore. When she came on softer ground where her tracks might be seen, she tore up her hands jerking a branch from a bush at the side of the trail. She dragged it behind her to erase her steps.

Under a cloudy sky, it was cool by day, but the nights were so cold with no blankets, she shivered as she hugged herself, afraid she was not going to survive.

Tears came often, but nothing could persuade her to return to a man who had killed a saloon woman. A man with a family she now hated because they had murdered her father. Dying in the mountains would be preferable to going back, but she kept praying for help.

Knowing she could no longer stay in the high terrain if she wanted to survive, she turned east and downhill through brush and jagged rocks, believing she would soon come down to the stage road.

*　　*　　*　　*　　*

Days later in the late afternoon on a Monday, a lone rider headed west among the high rolling hills, aiming for the distant stage road, which ran north and south on a narrow passage. The yellow and green dotted mountains rose to the west. A light wind blew under a cloudy sky. His chunky sorrel gelding seemed tireless on the dirt and sand. In the silence of the land, the creak of his saddle and hoof beats were the only sound.

He was Billy Tyson, twenty-five, and rode easy in the saddle. Tall and husky, he had dark brown, collar length hair and darker eyes with a diamond sparkle. Clean-shaven, ruggedly handsome, he wore range clothes with a black vest and a right-handed holster, tied down, with an Army colt. His wide brimmed Stetson shaded his sharp gaze.

Despite his calm, there was obviously something very dangerous about him.

Along with his bedroll and possible sack, Billy had a concertina—a squeeze-box accordion decorated in crimson and gold—dangling from the horn with his canteen.

Rounding the last hill, he spotted a big freight wagon pulled by a team of two bays headed north on the well-trod stage road. The wagon had white lettering on the sides of its canvas top: LINSTROM FREIGHT.

Driving the outfit was Red Linstrom, seventy-three, with a wiry, graying red beard, and gray hair with faded red tint. In blue jacket and shirt with tan britches, he sported a wide-brimmed tan hat with a many-colored braided band. He wore fancy black boots with blue trim at the tops. A Winchester repeating rifle leaned on the seat at his side.

With twinkling gray-blue eyes, Red looked like a friendly family man with arms open to the whole world. No hidden agenda, no secrets. Just a trader enjoying the sun and his way of life.

Under the wagon seat close to his boots lay his male border collie, medium-sized, and black with a white nose and collar. It was asleep.

When Red saw Billy riding toward him from the east, he drew his team to a halt. His dog, alerted, jumped up on the wagon seat.

Billy came up along side and reined short. He liked the trader on sight. Red had the same reaction. They grinned at each other.

Red nodded to the concertina. "Hi, young fellah. You play that thing?"

"Sure do."

"Well, tie up your pony. Glad for the company. I'm Red Linstrom."

"Billy Tyson."

Billy dismounted, loosened the cinch, and tied a lead rope to the rear of the wagon.

He came around and climbed up on the wagon seat to Red's left but couldn't sit down until Red moved his dog off and under his feet again. Billy had his concertina in hand.

Billy hesitated before sitting down when he saw the border collie.

"That's Kip," Red grinned as Billy settled next to him. "He lives in the wagon but he lets me hang out with him."

They shook hands. Red then slapped the lines and set the team moving.

Red grinned at Billy. "I saw you down in Mesilla a long time back. Playing games with some Mexican kids. And letting 'em win every time."

Billy nodded with an easy smile.

"Where you from, Billy? Where's your home?"

"It was West Texas."

"Got folks there?" Red saw the gloom as Billy shook his head. "Me, I come from Tennessee."

"What's that like?"

"Green and pretty. So, you been riding the grub line?"

Billy shrugged. "Sometimes. Working my way north."

"I was the same at your age. Took all kinds of jobs. Until someone pinned a badge on me. Wore it a lot of years until this pretty woman came along and hog-tied me. I hung it up and started a freight line to support her and the kids." He glanced at Billy. "How about you, got a girl?"

"No, sir."

"Don't you want to settle down some day?"

Billy shook his head. "Uh-uh."

"Afraid of responsibility?"

Billy grinned. "Afraid of women."

"Had two sons once, just like you, carefree and all." Red sobered with sudden gloom. "Lost 'em both at Shiloh."

"Sorry to hear that."

They were silent awhile. The dog had fallen asleep between them.

Billy pushed his hat back. "Meeting a friend at the next relay station."

"That's where I'm headed. Rhyker's Station on Wild Horse Flats."

Billy turned his face to hide his sudden grimness.

When they passed some brush on the left, a black-tailed jack rabbit darted up the road and then headed back toward the mountain. The dog, dozing, missed it. Overhead, a turkey buzzard spread it wings and floated across the sky until it darted east toward the hills.

Billy was so somber, Red tried to cheer him.

"You'll like Rhyker's," Red offered. "The station does more than service the stage line. Travelers and a lot of ranchers count on it for supplies. I have a few crates of apples from my wife, and Mrs. Rhyker makes apple pies you can smell a mile away."

As the wagon rolled north along the stage road, Billy began to play the concertina. The dog immediately sat up and wagged its tail.

Billy sang a traditional folk song in a clear strong voice.

"Oh, where have you been, Billy Boy, Billy Boy…"

Red's deep voice joined in. "Oh, where have you been, Charming Billy…"

Billy continued. "I have been to seek a wife, she's the darling of my life…"

Red added, "She's a young thing and cannot leave her mother…"

19

They laughed and continued the many verses together. As the wagon rolled north along the wagon road, the music rose in the wind with both men singing.

"How old is she, Billy Boy, Billy Boy,
How old is she, charming Billy,
Six times eight and four times seven,
Twenty eight and eleven,
She's a young thing and cannot leave her mother."

They laughed, and Billy felt at home.

"You play that thing pretty darn good," Red told him. "Who taught you?"

"My Pa." Billy winced in painful memory. "When you ride alone, it helps. And I write songs to pass the time."

"You write songs? Like what?"

"Like a good old-fashioned square dance," Billy said and played a lively tune as he sang:

"There was an old man with a wooden leg.
And he danced all night with a gal named Meg.
A woodpecker came and the fight was on,
Made the bird so tame, it danced right along."

Now the dog couldn't stand it any longer and howled with the music.

Red grinned and thought any man would want Billy for a son.

After Kip's howl got to be too much, Billy set aside his concertina. The dog settled back down, exhausted.

Red gestured at the rocky hills to their right as the day grew long. "We'll camp up ahead at nightfall. Seven Springs, it's a canyon where folks can rest and get water year round. There's a lot of other springs along the way in those canyons, but most of 'em will dry up before long."

Shadows grew long. They were shaded by the mountains as the sun lowered in the west beyond the cliffs. As the wagon rolled north, the terrain continued to rise with brush and rocks on both sides of the wide road and hid what awaited them around the turn.

"They widened this pass for the stage and cattle drives. Used a lot of dynamite," Red told Billy. "So you got the high mountains to the left and them high rocky hills to the right. When you get to the station, it just goes flat all the way north to the blue mountains."

Billy felt sleepy as Red filled him in on the country side. What was even more comfortable—he felt at home with the trader. A man much like Billy's dad, who he painfully remembered.

CHAPTER 2

Unseen by Billy and Red as the wagon rolled north on the stage road that Monday and toward evening, Jocelyn Miller Callahan was coming down the brushy slope of the mountains not far ahead. Torn and battered, exhausted, she fought to keep going downhill. The road lay below but it felt like she would never reach it.

Several hundred feet above and west of the road, Jocelyn hovered in the smelly creosote. Her long hair was matted and her face and hands scratched, but she was still incredibly beautiful even in her misery.

It was late in the day but with lingering sunshine, and she knew she would be exposed once she cleared the brush. She constantly looked back up at the ridges above her. She had seen riders up there when she was hiding in the rocks.

Still wearing her tattered, white wedding gown with shredded sleeves and hem, petticoat matted and torn around her ankles, she kept fighting her way down toward the road. Her soft shoes were nearly worn through.

She heard distant music coming from the south and below.

A chance, an escape, food, water—anyone but the trackers

on her trail. Half-crazed from lack of sustenance, her hands and ankles bloodied, Jocelyn staggered down through the rocks. The brush now was only knee deep.

Finding herself in the open all of a sudden, she could be seen from the ridges behind her to the west—and she was.

Up on the cliffs in the fading sunlight, two riders spotted her scrambling down toward the road before they lost sight of her. They started the rough ride on the steep grade down toward where they had seen her last.

Afraid of them, she hunched down in the brush but realized it was too late. After catching her breath, she rose and started down again. Snagged by bristles and thorns, she was tangled, forced to a halt while she freed herself.

Dear God, she silently prayed, *please help me!*

Coming down hundreds of feet above her and in the lead on a sorrel, Sid Callahan wore a sidearm, tied down. Sid had always fancied himself as a fast draw. It was in his upbringing that the Callahans were so powerful, they could get away with anything.

With him was Twigs, thirty-one, tall and lean on a tall bay horse. He wore a sidearm but looked as if he wouldn't even shoot a rattler. Riding the grub line up from Texas had brought him to the Callahan Ranch. He had stayed because they liked his skill with a rope and handling horses and cattle. Good-looking in a carefree way with an easy smile, he had dark brown eyes and hair.

At the same time, Red drove his wagon north around the bend but abruptly pulled the team to a halt. Billy, playing the concertina and seated at his side, his horse still trailing behind the outfit, shared his surprise and stopped the music.

Kip rose up, but Red put his hand on the dog's head. "Stay."

On the road now, some two hundred feet ahead, Jocelyn staggered toward them, her ragged wedding dress barely staying on her. Desperate, teary eyed, she raised her hand and signaled. Then she fell to her knees.

Red raised the lines, then stopped as he spotted the two riders.

Billy's gaze turned dark at seeing a woman in trouble. A young woman with long yellow hair. He bit his lip to stop himself from yelling.

Coming down the grade on her trail, Sid Callahan reached the road ahead of Twigs. He reined up and swung down from the saddle. He grabbed her arm and jerked her up and around.

Red grimaced. "Looks like the Miller girl. Her pa was county sheriff out of Three Wells. And that's Sid Callahan."

"From Texas?" Billy asked.

"Yeah, the whole clan come up here about ten years ago with a big herd."

Sid struggled with Jocelyn on the road ahead.

"Stop here," Billy said. He set aside his concertina and hurriedly jumped down. His blood running ice cold, his face hot, Billy dreaded the sound of any screams, yet she was not crying out.

Red warned him. "Watch out, Billy. He's real fast."

Red rested the lines, pausing to watch Twigs riding down the slope. Red reached for his Winchester and worked a shell into the chamber. He raised it to his shoulder.

Twigs stayed back from Sid and the girl, signaling to Red he'd not interfere, after which Red lowered his weapon.

As Sid Callahan wrestled with Jocelyn, Billy moved forward at a slow, deliberate pace, his eyes narrowed, his mouth tight.

Sid still struggled with Jocelyn until she bit his hand. He yelped, let go as she staggered back. Sid started after her again. She kicked him in the shins.

Angered, Sid slapped her so hard, she dropped down on her knees.

Billy, furious, came closer, now within forty feet. He bore no resemblance to the happy kid on the wagon. He looked like a man with death in his holster. He could not bear the sight of a woman in trouble. His heart beat faster. He felt sick to his insides.

Billy's voice was strong, icy. "Let her go."

Sid snarled. "Back off. She's my brother's wife."

Billy considered this and stopped briefly, then continued.

Sid grabbed her by the arm, yanked her to her feet. She cried out, kicked at him, tried to break free. Sid dragged her along toward his horse where it stood, so nervous it started backing away.

Now Billy was within less than twenty feet and stopped, needing the space if Sid drew on him.

Red, still on the wagon seat, kept his rifle hip high but leveled on Twigs.

Jocelyn struggled, bit Sid's left hand again, drawing blood.

Sid yelled. "Yow!" He slammed his fist into her jaw. Stunned, she crumbled, barely conscious. Sid kicked at her.

Billy's voice could be no colder. "Get away from her."

Sid looked from the fallen Jocelyn to the upstart who was getting to be annoying.

Billy took a stance. He stood with his right hand at his side by his holster.

Sid sneered. "Listen, sonny. She's going back with me."

"No!" Jocelyn cried as her eyes pleaded with Billy for help.

All the while, Red kept his rifle on Twigs, who was clearly not interested in getting involved.

But Twigs had to warn Sid. "Let it go, Sid, that's Billy Tyson. He's real fast."

Sid straightened. "Never heard of him."

"He'll take you down," Twigs said.

Sid Callahan didn't believe it, sneered.

Billy held his stance, feet spread. "Get on your horse and get out of here."

There was a tense moment as Sid stepped clear of Jocelyn and moved further into the road where he stopped, working his fingers near his right holster. "Slap leather or get."

Red waved his rifle. "Sid, you go on home."

"Old man, you just stay out of this." And to Billy, "You backing off, sonny?"

"No, you are." Billy looked all the more dangerous.

Sid enjoyed the moment. A runaway bride on the ground. An upstart facing him, about to die. Two spectators who would praise his courage, his speed, and his power. A story he could tell his father when he got back to the ranch.

Then suddenly, Sid started his draw.

Billy drew so fast, it stunned everyone. He aimed at Sid, but didn't fire.

Sid, revolver half out of his holster, hesitated in dismay. He stared into the barrel of Billy's six-gun. Sweat on his face, he was in a quandary. He could try to finish his draw and get shot, and he would surely die. He felt as if the bullet was already ripping through him.

Billy's face was dark with fury. "You can die now. Or we can talk about West Texas. And the Bonneville Ranch."

Sid didn't react to Texas or the Bonneville Ranch. He only knew that Billy's eyes burned like fire, like the devil himself about to be the end of Sid Callahan. Long hush as Sid saw death staring him in the face. He was so scared he felt his insides rumble.

Now of a sudden, Sid messed his britches. Loudly. He paled, turned ashen. He felt the clump and wet in his long johns, trickling down his leg. Shame turned his face from white to pink to red.

Sid let his six-gun slide back into the holster. He shivered, hands lifted.

Billy looked fierce. "Right hand in the air. Drop your gun belt."

Sid raised his right hand, dropped his gun belt with his left. He backed away, retreated to his horse, keeping his gaze on Billy even as he mounted. He looked real uncomfortable as he squirmed on the saddle. "This ain't over."

Red lowered his Winchester. Jocelyn sat trembling on the ground.

Sid, likely squishing in his britches, turned to Twigs. "Go find Pa. I'm going back to the ranch." Sid rode around the wagon and south on the road.

Billy holstered his Colt. He walked over to Twigs and took an offered canteen, which he then took to the battered girl, handing it down to her. His hands were shaking in anger. She could see fire in his gaze.

Barely alive, she yet managed a grateful smile as she took the canteen from him in her trembling, bleeding hands. She sank down a little and drank as if she hadn't had any water ever.

Billy could see she was hurting, but he didn't know what to do. She returned the canteen as she sat up a little more. He stood over her with the canteen in hand.

Red Linstrom had already stepped down with his rifle, walked around the wagon to make sure Sid kept going. Then he put his rifle back on the wagon seat with Kip. He hurried forward and over to kneel by the fallen Jocelyn, who sat shivering. He peeled off his coat and put it around her shoulders.

Billy backed away to where Twigs still sat on his horse.

Red lifted her to her feet, his arm around her. He half carried her as he walked her back to the wagon where they could not hear Billy and Twigs. She suddenly collapsed and sat down, Red kneeling with her near the front wheel. Above on the wagon front, Kip leaned out, then jumped down and came over to her. The dog licked her face until she smiled, after which Red pulled the dog away.

Red tried to get her up, but she wouldn't move away from the front wheel.

Still out of earshot, Twigs rode closer to Billy, who returned the canteen. Bending down, Billy picked up Sid's gunbelt and handed it up to Twigs. They spoke in low voices so they could not be heard.

"Ole Sid's never been treed before." Twigs grinned. "He's gone home to change his clothes." Sobered, he leaned forward, low to the cantle. "And I have to get back to Blair Callahan, but I'll take it slow."

"Where is he?"

"He's a day's ride, west of here, still looking for her on the prairie. Got Wiley with him."

"Wiley?"

Twigs nodded. "He's an old-time buffalo hunter old man Callahan hired as a tracker, but Wiley must be going blind. I saw signs he missed, which was fine with me, so I just went along with him. But then, Sid and me, we were up on the ridge by ourselves hunting for the girl when he lucked out by spotting her way below."

Billy and Twigs gazed at each other a long, careful moment.

"You're riding a dangerous trail." Billy said.

"Yeah, but I still don't have any proof."

"We ruled out most everyone else."

Twigs nodded. "Blair is the big he-bull in this territory, just like in Texas. He only knows one way—his. Sid is a killer and proud of it, but you shamed him, so he'll want to get even. And Jody, that girl's husband, is a pansy. I haven't met Pike Callahan, but I hear he was at the wedding. He's Blair's brother. From up north somewhere. I heard he has a mine, and no interest in ranching, so the spread belongs to Blair."

"We need time to get her safe."

"I'll take as long as I can. But it's for sure when Blair learns where she is, he'll come after her with an army."

"We're headed for Rhyker's. Be there tomorrow."

"Yeah, I know I was to meet you there, but now I may be

riding with Blair. I figure we'll be two or three days behind you."

They were both conscious of Jocelyn and Red over at the wagon, still out of earshot. They could see her refusing or unable to stand up, with Red kneeling at her side.

Twigs and Billy did not shake hands by design.

"That girl," Twigs said, "she can't go back to them."

"I know."

"You can't see how really beautiful she is," Twigs added.

"Yes, I can."

They hesitated as painful memories rose between them.

Twigs tipped his hat to her from the distance, waved to Red, turned his horse, and rode back up the high ground and west into the mountains. He entered a canyon pass and was soon sheltered by rocks and brush.

Billy watched until Twigs was out of sight before returning to the wagon. It was already twilight. He felt stiff and numb. He could not move for a long while. He had come close to killing a man, a stranger, and yet perhaps a man deserving to die.

Near the front wheel, Jocelyn still sat on the ground with Red's coat around her. He was kneeling at her side. She looked like she might not survive. Shivering, bleeding on her hands and ankles with her clothes torn, she seemed barely alive.

Red's dog Kip leaned close to her as if her protector.

Billy walked slowly over to them.

Red looked up at Billy. "I made room in the back of the wagon. Got her set up with some bread and a canteen. And blankets. Now we got to get her in there so she can rest up. I can't do the lifting. Not anymore."

Billy bent down, lifted her into his arms, straightened to stand with her. She felt light, cold, yet all woman. Never in his young life had he lifted a woman into his arms. It was an amazing experience that shook him down to his boots. At the same time, he ached for her suffering.

Her head rolled against his shoulder as she clung to him. He carried her around to the back of the wagon where his horse was still on a lead. Red had lowered the two foot high tail gate and made a wide space for her. Freight was stacked around the spot.

Billy tried to set her in the wagon, but she clung to him, wouldn't let go, her face at his throat. She shivered, trembled. Billy had no idea what to do. He wanted to protect her, make life better for her, keep her safe.

"Come now, child," Red coaxed her. "It's getting dark."

Billy could do nothing to move her. She remained clamped onto him.

"I'm Red Linstrom," the freighter told her. "This here's Billy Tyson. We're headed for the relay station, be there tomorrow. Mrs. Rhyker will take care of you, but we got to get there first."

Red retrieved one of the blankets. He tried to wrap it around her, but she would not let go of Billy.

"Please, honey child," Red pleaded. "There's a campground up the next canyon. It's called Seven Springs. Has a pond. We'll camp there, get some food in you. You can get freshened up. And we'll find something for you to wear in my freight."

Finally, she let Billy set her beyond the tailgate and move her into the wagon. He pulled the blankets around her. She settled back with a sweet smile of thanks even though she had tears in her eyes.

She whimpered. "They'll come after me."

Red shook his head. "They'll be days catching up with us. And they won't be getting their hands on you, we promise."

At that point, Kip tried to jump up on the tailgate. Red picked the dog up and set him in with her. Kip immediately crawled next to her, and she put her arm about him.

"Dogs always know trouble," Red said with a brief smile as he sought to comfort her. "Tonight, we'll get you fixed up with what

I can find in here, and outfitted at Ryker's. Then we'll see about getting you on the north-bound. I don't know how often it runs of late."

Red raised the tailgate, and she settled back.

Billy and Red returned to climb up on the wagon seat. Red slapped the lines to start the team. Long shadows crossed their path in the twilight.

Red glanced at Billy. "Fast as you are, how come I never heard of you?"

Billy, still somber, just shrugged.

"Ever shoot anyone?" Red asked carefully.

Billy shook his head, staring at the shadows. No, but years of practice had sped his hand faster and faster, until it was like a streak of lightning. His fury at Sid's treatment of the girl had kept him from any hesitation. He had to help her, save her. It was what a man had to do.

Red flipped the lines to urge the team onward. "You had him cold, so you're no killer, but you sure wanted to pull that trigger."

Billy shrugged while staring off into the shadows.

"Well, you're in for it now." Red thought a moment. "I guess we all are."

They moved on in silence. The creaking of the harness, hoof beats and a howl from a distant coyote were the only sounds.

In the back of the wagon, wrapped in her blankets in near darkness, Jocelyn could not hear their conversation. She lay quiet, hugging Kip to her side for comfort. It had all happened so fast. Staggering down to the road, being grabbed by Sid, beaten and falling to the ground. Watching a young man with gleaming eyes march to her rescue. Seeing Sid's bravado and fearing for the stranger's life. Then seeing that amazing speed of a draw that left Sid terrified that he was going to die.

She knew Sid had messed his britches. That meant he would not rest until he took revenge on the stranger. Red's comfort had taken her to the wagon where she had collapsed. She had felt safe for the moment. But nothing could compare to having her rescuer lift her in his arms. Feeling the strength, the power, the joy of his embrace. She had wanted to stay that way forever, held and protected from the Callahans.

That night in the mouth of a wooded canyon on the side of the road, camp was made with a blazing fire to offer hot food and coffee to Jocelyn. Clouds moved across the starry sky. The moon was low on the horizon.

The howl of coyotes rang far away.

A little varmint scooted behind a cottonwood and up through the brush.

Jocelyn, freshly bathed as best she could, now wore a blue print dress with high collar and long sleeves, along with a jacket, which Red had found in the freight for a mercantile. She had new shoes. He had supplied her with a comb and towels.

Her hair now soft around her shoulders, she looked like she would survive. Covered with blankets and sitting against a saddle, she sipped coffee and gladly accepted a plate of beans. The dog stayed close to her.

She was so beautiful now, it unnerved Billy. He had stationed himself near the road, out of the firelight and away from the wagon and horses. His back to them, he sat on a rock with a Winchester resting on his knees. He could hear their conversation.

On a vengeance trail for most of his young life, he had never thought of having a family of his own, not until now. He figured he would never luck out with such a lovely young woman, because he had nothing to offer. His horse and saddle, a rifle and six-gun, and a concertina. She could do better, but it was causing him to think about land of his own, and more.

Back at the fire, Jocelyn often glanced toward Billy and thought, *Lord, thank you for these men. Thank you for Billy. He's my hero. I think I love him.*

The fire crackled with white and yellow flames, smelling homey in the night.

Red sat near her. "So, you must have had a good reason to run away."

She winced. "Yes, it was during the wedding reception at the ranch, late at night. I overheard Sid and his father. They said Jody, my husband, had killed a saloon girl, and how my father was going to arrest Jody, and it was Sid who shot him in the back."

"My God," Red responded. "No wonder you left."

"I was afraid."

"How long have you been out in the wild?"

"I don't know. Maybe a week or more. My horse ran off a few days ago. Left me without food or water."

"Where were you headed?"

"I have an aunt in St. Louis. She won't want anything to do with me, but maybe she'd help me just to get rid of me."

"We'll get you on your way. And don't you worry about paying for anything. This country owes you."

She smiled, grateful, and set her cup aside.

Billy had heard her story and now returned to sit by the fire, opposite them.

Red waved him to sit near where his concertina rested on his saddle. "Play us a tune, Billy."

Billy hesitated but he relented and retrieved his concertina. He whipped up a soft ballad and had barely started when the dog rose up and began to howl along with it. Red had trouble getting the animal to quiet down, after which Kip curled up next to Jocelyn once again.

Billy played into the night. If he stopped playing, she would begin to awaken. He became afraid to stop the music until she no longer stirred.

As chivalrous as Red, but for his own painful reasons, Billy watched as she slept with the firelight dancing on her flaxen hair and the dog next to her side.

Finally, Billy set aside his concertina.

Red fussed and whispered. "We can't let the Callahans take her back."

Billy put more wood onto the fire. "No, we can't," he murmured. He took up his rifle, preparing to stay on guard.

"Wake me at midnight." Red lay back in his blankets, close to the fire.

Billy nodded, turned, and gazed a long while at the sleeping, beautiful young girl.

Then he stood with his concertina and rifle. He walked out of the firelight to stand guard by the road. He heard a lone coyote howling at the moon. It echoed new thoughts stirring in Billy's heart. 'Lord, help me to protect this girl, get her to safety. And if it be thy will, maybe she'll look on me kindly. Not as just a man with a gun.'

Despite his prayers, he knew the nightmares would never go away, not until he could set things right.

As he looked up at the stars, a song formed in his thoughts and he put it to words, as he often had over the years, but now he only played the ballad and didn't sing aloud, only in his heart.

> *And there she was, so young and fair,*
> *With eyes of blue and golden hair...*

He fumbled with further lines because it would not only be painful, but mark an even bigger divide between them. It would be a story of a man on a vengeance trail, a man who could die if he failed. Not a man for a lass like her.

Yes, Billy knew Jocelyn deserved better, but he yearned to be the one she chose. Over the years, he had met others, but not one of them had penetrated his buried anger. It had taken Jocelyn's shining eyes to reach inside of him and stir up feelings he didn't know he had.

He lowered the canteen and looked skyward. "Lord, help me find my way."

At daybreak on Tuesday at Seven Springs under a clear sky, Red had more beans in the iron frying pan. Coffee steamed on hot coals near the flames. Billy returned from standing guard at the wagon. It was cold and quiet.

Jocelyn looked refreshed, less afraid. She sat in her blankets against the saddle and enjoyed breakfast and coffee. Her hair combed, face brighter, she looked lovely.

Billy poured himself a cup of coffee and took a plate of beans. He sat back, away from her. Red had already eaten and was feeding his dog until Kip left him and returned to lie at Jocelyn's side.

Red sat back and sipped his coffee. "Callahans are a rough outfit."

She nodded. "Jody's a lot younger than his brother, and they always give him anything he wants. I guess that includes me."

"I heard Blair had an older brother," Red remarked.

"Yes, Pike. Jody said once that when he was a kid, both Blair and Pike had had some really bad trouble with squatters and that's when Pike left to go north to live. In Montana. But he came back for the wedding."

"He look like Blair?" Red asked.

"He came late, after the ceremony, but I had only a glimpse of him that night when he was on the porch. It was dark. I could see he was bigger than Blair but that's all." Billy was shaken by the mention of squatters. He got up, walked closer to the road, and stood with his back to them. He continued to listen but his face was hot. Repressed anger burned in his gaze. Inside his inner turmoil, he now believed more than ever the Callahans had to have led the raid in West Texas. Proving it, though, could be near impossible.

But, he thought, *maybe Pike went north right after the raid to hide his broken hand, so no lawman would look at the windlass and figure it out. And maybe he was also ashamed of how his hand ended up.*

At the same time, he worried all the more about Jocelyn. Never again in his life did he want to hear a woman's scream. Especially her. She must never be taken away by the Callahans. He was willing to give his life to make sure that never happened.

Red remained by the fire with her and refilled their cups. He could see how she kept gazing toward Billy. They knew he was listening.

"I only met your father once, but he seemed like an upright fellow," Red told her. "And you sure had a rough time of it. But why a Callahan?"

She settled down and sipped her coffee. "I lost my mother when I was five, and then my father last year. I was lonely with only my aunt back East who doesn't want me. And Jody was so sweet. But I didn't know he was the reason my father had died."

Red sipped his coffee and waited for her to continue.

"Not until the reception at the Callahan Ranch that night. There was too much drinking and smoking inside the house. It was loud and crowded. So much smoke and liquor, I couldn't breathe. And I was already sorry I had married Jody, but it was too late."

Red was silent. Billy could hear but didn't turn.

Jocelyn brushed away a tear. "I walked outside, alone, down in the rose garden. It was dark. And then I heard voices somewhere nearby, but they couldn't see me. It was Sid and his father. When I heard how Jody had killed a woman, and why my father was murdered, to keep Jody from hanging, I knew I had to get away. But I was afraid to go back inside to change or get anything at all, because I knew they'd stop me. So I just took a horse and left."

"You were brave," Red told her.

"Maybe foolish, but I thought if I could circle north through the mountains and then get on the stage road, I might have a chance. It was God's blessing that you and Billy had come along. And that Billy could stop Sid, something I never thought could happen." She paused to sip her coffee. "But I know they'll try to get me back. For Jody."

"And because you could get them hanged?" Red suggested.

She wiped a tear from her left cheek. "No one would believe me, not against them."

"Well, it's for sure they'll figure where we're headed."

"Yes, and now I've got the two of you in trouble." She glanced over toward Billy, who didn't turn.

"Don't worry," Red assured her. " Nobody's getting between you and Billy. Or me. And Rhyker's a good man, a tough hombre. Got himself a tough Apache wife. Mescalero. She won't let nobody give you no trouble."

"Thank you," she said, all the more grateful. "And thank you for the dress. It will always be my favorite."

As Billy returned for more coffee, she smiled up at him. "You were the brave one."

Red grinned. "Nah, he's a kid, and they just ain't too smart."

They shared a soft laugh, but Billy, embarrassed, poured himself a steaming cup before turning away. He walked over to the horses and was now out of ear shot.

She worried. "Is he blaming me for all this?"

Red downed his coffee. "No, honey. That kid carries his own misery, whatever it is."

She nodded. "I could tell he wanted to kill Sid so bad, his hand was turning white."

"When Sid put his fist in your face, I figure that was a little too much for Billy."

"No, it was more than that. He looked like the left hand of God."

"Yeah, maybe so. But don't you worry, honey, you're not alone anymore."

Tears trickled down her face as she smiled her thanks. She looked again toward Billy with growing affection for the wild young gunslinger, and not just for gratitude. He would be so easy to love, at least from a distance. She felt somehow her father would have liked him.

Both men had touched her heart, and the dog offered its own comfort.

But it was Billy she wanted to hug forever.

CHAPTER 3

A fter breakfast at the Seven Springs campground, Red got busy with harnessing his team to his freight wagon, as his dog danced around him under a clear sky.

Billy was further back and saddling his sorrel.

Jocelyn stopped to touch Red's arm, then turned and shyly came over to Billy. "Thank you," she said. "You saved my life, you and Mr. Linstrom."

Embarrassed, Billy could not tell her that she was not the only reason he had taken on a Callahan. Yet, saving her had given him more pleasure than he had ever had. He could still feel her soft and vulnerable in his arms. *A man would enjoy that any time*, Billy thought, *forever, if he could.*

On her part, Jocelyn could still feel the horror of Sid trying to take her prisoner. Even more so, she could see Billy facing him down with a gun in his hand. Nor could she forget the strength of Billy's arms and how he had smelled of leather.

"Are you going with us to the station?" she asked, hopefully.

Billy nodded as he tightened the cinch. He had already decided he would stay long enough to protect her, no matter how long it took. She was not going back to the Callahans.

Red came over to them, his dog at his heels. "Miss Jocelyn, you can ride up front with me."

His dog jumped up on the wagon seat, but Red caught him and set him on high.

Jocelyn smiled at Red and took his arm. "I'm so grateful to you and Billy."

"You're in good hands now," Red promised as he led her forward. He helped her climb up on the wagon seat where she could sit to his left as he drove. The dog settled between them.

Billy mounted his horse. Haunted by her blue eyes, he thought of his mother, who had the same and lots of golden hair, just like Jocelyn's. His mother would say that this girl was his passage to leave the past behind for a better life. How he wished she was here to say it, to lecture him about coming inside with muddy boots, to scold him for not doing his lessons, and to hug and kiss him goodnight. She had always smelled of soap and spice and roses.

His mother would also tell him to pursue Jocelyn.

Billy brushed the thought aside, because he could not look beyond finding the killers and ensuring they faced a reckoning. Anything further, he could only pray for that which he now yearned, a new life.

While Red's outfit made ready to get back on the stage road, Twigs was on the move in the far west. He had camped out in the mountains and now traveled at a slow pace. He rode down onto the flats and continued west.

He thought of Billy's incredible fast draw and how Billy had changed from a happy boy to a dangerous man. Like Billy, Twigs prayed for the reckoning, and for a better life.

Soon he spotted a camp on the prairie, just south of the mountains and near a little creek that eventually trickled into the sand.

He heard the soft sound of a harmonica playing a ballad.

Two men were there, standing by the flickering fire. Twigs reined short and dismounted, taking time to loosen the cinch and leave his horse with the others. He had a story to tell, but he'd have to do it without getting shot. Containing his grin was so hard, he took his time to get sober before walking over to the fire.

Potluck, short and dumpy and pushing forty, lowered his rifle. A man who would do anything for Blair Callahan, Potluck told himself he would even kill for him, but so far, had avoided having to pull the trigger. In truth, he didn't have the guts because he didn't want to get shot in return.

Standing back and pocketing his harmonica, the eighty-year-old bearded Wiley had all the looks of an old buffalo hunter, a mountain man who could live off the land. He even had his big Sharps rifle resting on his saddle on the ground and back from the fire. He wore buckskins, always bragging that a lovely Indian maid had chewed them soft for him. He had a hat with a floppy brim and an eagle feather stuck in his hat band.

Wiley was not a killer. He had long ago given up hunting buffalo for the railroad because of increasing aches and pains. He had turned down offers to scout for the army. He had lost his Cheyenne wife years back to a fever. He had no children, and he was alone, probably forever. He rode for the brand because he was tired of being on his own in the mountains and needed a home, such as it was. Blair Callahan asked nothing of him except to track rustlers and mountain lions.

The morning sun was bright, and no wind to speak of.

Twigs knelt to pour some coffee. "I thought old man Callahan was with you."

Wiley shrugged. "Left yesterday to check on Jody back at the ranch. You spot the girl?"

"Yeah, on the stage road with some old timer's freight wagon.

Name on it was Linstrom."

Wiley nodded. "Red Linstrom."

Potluck fussed. "You let her go?"

"Had no choice," Twigs said.

"What do you mean, no choice?" Potluck persisted.

"Where's Sid?" Wiley asked, ignoring Potluck.

Twigs tried to look sober. "Gone back home."

Wiley sat cross legged and poured himself some coffee. "What happened?"

Twigs squatted nearby with his own cup. He struggled against breaking into a grin. "Sid got to her on the stage road. She was on foot. The wagon was coming up from the south. Sid was fighting with her. But some kid got in his way." Twigs let it sink in. "Billy Tyson."

Potluck grunted. "Never heard of him."

Twigs took his time. "It was a standoff for a bit. But then ole Sid put his fist in the girl's face."

Wiley sipped his coffee. "That's rotten."

Twigs nodded. "She was already torn up from being on foot in the mountains, and with Sid beating on her, that was too much for Billy."

Potluck made a face. "Yeah?"

Finally, Twigs had to grin. "Ever see a rattlesnake sunning itself, real peaceful? Then throw a rock at it and see what you get? That's Billy Tyson."

Potluck walked closer to the fire. "Get on with it."

"They were going to draw on each other."

"No one's faster than Sid," Potluck snickered.

Twigs sat back, took his time and savored his coffee before continuing.

"Things got hot. Sid went for his gun first off, but Billy was faster." Twigs paused for effect. "Ole Sid, his Colt was only half out of the holster. He was staring right at Billy's. Now Billy could have shot him dead, but he took his time. I mean a lot of time."

Potluck snarled in disbelief. "You're lying."

Twigs took a moment to set aside his coffee and savored some beans. "Ole Sid, he just up and backed off. He was white as snow. And he left for home with his tail between his legs."

There was a long moment as the story hung in the air.

"I don't believe you," Potluck snapped.

"His gunbelt's on my saddle horn," Twigs said, gesturing.

Finally, Potluck pushed his hat back, glared at Twigs. "You better not repeat that story to anyone else. And what's more, where were you all this time?"

"Looking down that old man's rifle barrel. I figure they was headed for the relay station on Wild Horse Flats. Rhyker's. So I come back to make my report."

Wiley shook his head in thought as he hid his amusement.

"We got Hardy at Rhyker's," Potluck said. "Watching for her."

Potluck was steaming, pacing, wiping his mouth, dreading any kind of failure of Sid because Blair was a tough and nasty tyrant. He knew the old man loved his sons, but this meant trouble. A lot of it, and Potluck wanted to make sure he was out of the line of fire. He would never repeat any of this, not him.

Wiley stood up with his coffee and yawned. "I reckon we'd best head for the ranch. Callahan is going to want to call the shots. He may not want any trouble at the relay station. Wouldn't make him too popular. Everyone within a hundred miles depends on Rhyker's for supplies."

Potluck, mumbling to himself, stalked off. He claimed his horse and started to saddle up, away from them and out of earshot. He pushed on the rump of Wiley's big white mule, Lightning, which didn't budge aside but laid his long ears back. Potluck grumbled under his breath. The mule was taller than most of the horses and chunky. He was also stubborn, ornery, bite happy and could outrun Potluck's own mount. If Potluck was a little braver, he'd beat on the animal, but he knew Lightning would retaliate.

Meanwhile, Wiley followed Twigs as he led his horse down to the creek, knowing Twigs was holding something back. Wiley could read his friend and ached to know what Twigs was choking on as they walked.

Unheard by Potluck, they moved to the water's edge where the horse began to drink. Twigs couldn't hold back any longer and spoke in a low voice.

"It was really something to see. Sid went for his gun first, but he was already staring at Billy's. Never seen anyone draw so fast."

"Wish I had seen that."

Twigs chuckled. "Sid thought for sure he was gonna die. Billy just aimed and waited and waited, until Sid, well he went and messed his britches real bad. That's why he gave up and went home, so he could change his clothes."

Wiley bent down behind Twigs' horse, lifted a hoof to pretend he was checking the shoe. Blocked from Potluck's view and muffled by the rushing creek, Wiley kept his mouth tight over his chuckles.

Twigs turned his back to the campfire to hide his own grin.

For a moment they fought off their stifled laughter.

Wiley coughed. "Stink did he?"

"To high heaven."

Once Wiley found a way to hide his humor, he stroked Twig's mount and became curious. "So, what do you know about this Billy Tyson?"

"He's from Texas, that I heard. And he plays a squeeze box."

Wiley brightened. "A concertina? He can't be all bad."

*　　*　　*　　*　　*

Rhyker's Station lay on Wild Horse Flats, west of the stage road. Palo verde and mesquite in bloom spread all golden to the western grassland. Ahead, silver sage and red-dusted sand rolled north on flat prairie land to where blue mountains lined the far horizon.

Opposite the station to the east and some one hundred feet away across the road, a long rise of brush and rocks stood some ten feet high most of the way across but rocky in spots to 14 feet. It was about forty feet from side to side, obviously cut for the roadway. Behind the rise, a wide gully, then high, rolling, steep, wooded hills. North of it and the station, the land lay flat in all directions.

On the south side of the station, it was only forty feet to where a solid granite wall rose hundreds of feet high on the mountain side. It was rocky ground and useless as a road. Much of the rock piles had been shoved off the stage road itself, at least.

Tuesday's morning sun came with a light wind under a clear sky.

The station, a long rambling building, had walls fortified by adobe up to the windows, which had heavy shutters. Rifle slots were cut from the inside along all the walls. The depot, rooms for travelers, and a general store shared the large interior. It sported a long covered porch in front, but only a small porch in the rear of the station, leaving the back windows high off the ground.

"This is my home till I die," Rhyker often said.

On the north side, a ramp led up to a doorway to the storage room on the main floor, while below the building and between the porches, there was a shallow basement for cool storage, entered only from the north side.

On the high, front porch, which had a full roof and strong rails, there were benches against the walls. Off to the sides, there were crates in stacks.

A big trough and hitching rails were in front.

"No one comes in my kitchen," many had heard Rhyker's Apache wife tell them while holding a cleaver.

North side of the station building and a few hundred feet away, stood a long, single-level barn that held equipment and had some stalls. There was a tack room and bunkhouse on it's east side and next to the smithy.

Facing the station, the smith had a roof and a back wall, sides open with a low barrier. A trough stood ready on the east side. Corrals were further back and held more than a dozen coach horses and a half dozen others for riding. Back of the corrals were sheds of various sizes and the north barn.

Some distance behind and west of the station, there were two necessaries—one for ladies and one for gents—because Rhyker's Apache wife refused to provide or handle chamber pots.

"Not in my house," she had said.

Further north behind the station and set back, there stood a water tank on a platform. Nearby was an adobe-lined well and a creaky windmill turning slowly in the wind. Surface pipes ran to the house and also to the corral troughs.

A trading post as well as a relay, the station serviced travelers and local ranchers as well as farmers, providing hay and grain, for hundreds of miles around, saving them a week-long trip to town. They always took time for Rhyker's wife's hearty meals.

"Best beef steaks and apple pie west of the Mississippi," many would say.

On that Tuesday afternoon, the southbound stage came into view, dust rising. It seemed to rock from side to side as if broken.

Hardy, a gunman in his late forties, came out of the station and onto the front porch in the shade of the roof. He wore slick dark clothes and a low slung, tied down holster. He had a mustache and cold, gray eyes. He looked void of feelings or any deep thought, a man who wore his six-gun like a badge. A man who elevated himself by stepping on others. He knew old man Callahan set a lot of store by him.

"A killer by nature," it was often said of Hardy.

Hardy watched the southbound stage rocking crazily as it came to a noisy halt in front of the station. It continued to rock several times before settling with a loud cracking noise. The team of six were winded, run with sweat.

In his seventies, Hal Mintz, the driver, looked exhausted. With a trim white beard and mustache, wearing a tan duster over his shirt and britches, he sat with the lines in his hand as if unable to move. He loved every minute of his job, even when there was trouble, because he loved traveling in wondrous scenery and being on the move, but this time, he was badly shaken. They had come far too close to hurtling down the mountain trail to a bad finish.

Seated on the driver's left, Henry Marks, early fifties, was chunkier, clean-shaven, and holding a shotgun as if he couldn't let go. A former lawman, he fit the job. No one who knew him ever messed with him, and their runs were more free of highwaymen than most, but this was his last run. He had a wife and newborn son waiting for him in Texas.

Mintz turned to Marks and took a deep breath. "We made it."

"I'll never sell you short again," Marks said, pushing his hat back. "I think you can do just about anything with a team of horses."

"This time," Mintz admitted, "it was God's will."

Right then, Joe Rhyker came outside and onto the porch. In his sixties and husky, he was clean-shaven and wearing a long, heavy apron. He wore a big grin and waved to them.

Rhyker, a good man, tried to carry the world on his shoulders, and it was ever visible in his expression. He ignored Hardy, who remained watchful over to his left. Rhyker moved down the steps to stare at the crooked stance of the stage.

Marks swung down as Mintz remained in charge of the lines

and grinned down at Rhyker, if only because the stage had reached the station in one piece.

Mintz gestured. "The hitch was half busted when we ran over some rocks coming down the grade. Cracked the axle and tore up the undercarriage. Team got spooked. And no way we could fix it out there. So we're right lucky to be here."

Rhyker could see part of the damage. "Wow."

"Yeah," Mintz said. "I figure our passengers are upside down in there."

Chauncey, Rhyker's middle-aged and grizzly helper, limping from a game left leg and hunched with a bad right shoulder, came from the corrals to take over the team. Chauncey's injuries were from the War Between the States when he fought with the north. With him, Chipper, a young Mexican orphan in his teens who had been dropped off by some wagons traveling through over two years ago, did most of the heavy lifting.

Chauncey looked over the traces as if he wanted to free the team.

Mintz leaned down."Hold on, Chauncey. No change of horses just yet. After we unload, I need to take the coach over to the smithy first, so we can work on it. The whole undercarriage was busted coming down the grade."

Chauncey paused for a good look at the crooked frame. He shook his head in disbelief that it had held together this long.

Mintz secured the lines, swung off the coach and onto the ground. He rested a moment, then went forward of the team to speak with Rhyker and Marks, who were now surveying the harness.

Chauncey went round to greet the passengers. He dropped the steps and opened the door on the right side of the stage which faced the station itself. "Looks like we're going to have to put you folks up for awhile. You'll have your luggage soon's we unload the mail and some freight in the boot."

First out, forty-year-old Peter Potts. He wore a fancy blue vest with a dark store-bought suit but no duster, which left him covered with red dust. He had a small brimmed hat. He was paunchy, wore round spectacles, and used a cane. He may have been a good-looking man were he not such a pain. He snapped at Chauncey in a distinct Boston accent and unnecessary airs.

"This is an outrage," Potts said. "I'm going to report this."

Chauncey reacted. "You can thank your lucky stars your driver could handle the lines, or you'd be at the bottom of that mountain in one nice little heap."

Potts was in a huff and about to grumble something more when he saw the grim look on Chauncey's face. He didn't know Chauncey was thinking how wearing blue in the War had not been with the intention of protecting saps like this one.

Potts backed off in a snit. "This could never happen in Boston."

Chauncey waited until Potts moved aside.

Potts looked up to the porch where Nellie, a lovely Mescalero in her forties, was now standing and waving to her husband, Rhyker, who stood with Mintz and Marks on the other side of the lead horses where Mintz was checking some that appeared to have injury to their front legs.

Nellie wore a print dress, colorful sash, and moccasins. Slim and beautiful with her long black hair pulled back, she had a smile that always wrapped itself around her husband. Behind her dark eyes was more wisdom than could be found in most of the whites moving in her world. She was also more in tune with nature and faith than it appeared.

Potts sneered up at her after she went back inside and muttered, "What's that squaw doing here?"

Chauncey held his temper and spoke low. "Be glad Mr. Rhyker didn't hear you. That's his wife. Full-blooded Mescalero. She's also the cook, and unless you want to end up with a real belly ache, or maybe wake up some night without any hair, I'd watch my step."Potts grumbled and headed toward the steps with his cane swinging, then stopped to clear his glasses with his handkerchief.

Chauncey helped the other passenger step down. Eloise Perimenter was in her forties. She was pretty, slim, and blonde. Wearing a small hat and a duster over her traveling dress, she was a life-long ranch woman and weary of travel. And obviously of Peter Potts' blustering. As she saw him posturing near the porch steps, she muttered under her breath, "Fat head."

Chauncey heard her and grinned. He then went to help Chipper unload the coach. Chipper handled the shipments and luggage while Chauncey supervised.

Potts and Eloise made it onto the porch under the shade of the roof, but stopped to watch Chipper carry the baggage, one at a time, up the stairs. Their luggage sat waiting while Chipper stacked some of the small crates over on the north side of the porch where others, much larger, were already in a row.

Mintz, with Rhyker's help, carried the mail bag and strong box up onto the porch, then inside. The station was not an official post office but did have clearance from some ranchers to claim their incoming letters. They returned shortly, but did not offer to carry in the luggage as they hurried down to the coach and possibly-crippled team.

Eloise didn't hesitate and carried her two carpet bags inside. Potts grumbled as he picked up his bags, including a heavy sample case of his wares.

Inside the station, the vast front room had several round tables with six chairs each set near the big, dirty front windows. In the rear of the room, there was a long cluttered store counter facing them. Off to the right was the big storage room which also had an outside freight entrance.

Between the counter's low entry gate and the storage room, the kitchen was set back behind swinging doors. The aroma of strong coffee wafted from within.

To the far left of the front door, an opening led to a hallway, along which were lined guest rooms from front to back. The hallway also led to the rear of the station where Rhyker's quarters were next to the back exit door, which had narrow windows on either side of it.

Nellie, cold toward Potts, assigned the passengers their rooms. A hot meal was to be waiting for them, after they had freshened up. She liked Eloise at first glance, but she frowned because she could read Potts inside and out. A fop, a dandy, a fool, and a lot of trouble. If she had her way, the Boston man would sleep in the barn.

Out on the front porch, Hardy, Callahan's hired gun, went to the railing. He glared down at where Rhyker and Mintz, the driver, were now checking under the coach. Then he went back to sit on a bench near the front door and watch.

Rhyker backed away from the hitch. "Geez, I don't know how you made it."

"I did a lot of praying," Mintz replied.

Mintz climbed up on the coach, drove it in a circle and off to the smithy with Chipper and Chauncey following on foot. Mintz left them at the work shop to do the unhitching and start repair and walked back to the station.

Rhyker stood by the road in front of the station with Marks as Mintz joined them.

"Who's the hard case up there?" Mintz asked in a low voice.

"That's Hardy. One of Callahan's hired guns," Rhyker muttered. "Never misses a meal. Been staying on a cot in the tack room, since my wife won't put him up in the station. And Chauncey's locked down the bunkhouse."

"Looks like he's pretty sure of himself. Why is he here?" Marks asked.

Rhyker shrugged. "Whatever it is, he can't be up to any good."

"Maybe he's waiting for the northbound?" Mintz asked.

"Not due for a week." Rhyker said. "They cut back because of the Mescaleros. But we haven't see any. Have you?"

"No, but it doesn't mean they aren't there."

"Well, we know Hardy's not waiting on them," Rhyker added.

They stood a moment, pondering what Hardy's purpose might be. Everyone knew Blair Callahan ran rough-shod over this part of the territory and made everyone in town very nervous. Especially since no one had replaced the murdered county sheriff. Each election had had no takers. And it was two hundred miles to a U.S. Marshal.

Inside, at one of the tables that Tuesday afternoon, Potts sat facing Eloise as Nellie served them flapjacks and coffee. A tough woman, Nellie took no nonsense from anyone.

"I don't like hot cakes," Potts said. "Especially this time of day."

Nellie took back his plate. "Then you don't eat."

Potts stared up at her blazing dark brown eyes. He shriveled and reached to take back his plate. She made him struggle to take it, and then she turned her back and headed to the kitchen.

Eloise tried not to giggle. She had put up with this unpleasant man for over a week. She only sat with him because no one else would. Besides, his grumbling sometimes tickled her. She would have stories to tell when she was back home in Texas. Like the bug that flew in his mouth while on the open road. Or when he didn't quite make it to the stunt junipers to do his thing on the mountain road.

Potts grunted. "The bed is hard as a rock. Not even a chamber pot."

Again, Eloise fought not to laugh. She dug into her breakfast. "I love these flapjacks," she said.

Potts, his glasses always steaming up, just muttered to himself.

Nearby at another table, Mintz, Marks, Chauncey and Chipper, were enjoying their meal. Rhyker was behind the counter. Hardy sat alone in open threat.

*   *   *   *   *

While Mintz, Chauncey and Chipper continued working on the stage through late Tuesday afternoon, and while Red Linstrom's wagon headed north toward the station on a slight up grade with Billy and Jocelyn, Twigs helped break camp south of the mountains.

With Potluck in the lead with the pack horse, Twigs and Wiley trailed. They headed away from the ridges in the north mountain range, moving south on the prairie toward the far distant headquarters of the vast Callahan ranch.

At one point, they startled a half dozen prong horn antelopes, which darted west in a flash of tan and white, moving so fast they were soon just a stream of dust.

Wiley grunted to Twigs. "I hate that folks're hunting them down."

Twigs nodded. "Yeah, they are kind of pretty."

"This is their land," Wiley said. "Not ours."

Twigs nodded. He liked Wiley and the way the old timer felt close to nature. Though not so the red-tailed hawk that circled, looking for unwary rodents. Wiley had a thing for little varmints.

Potluck rode in the lead, out of earshot, leading the pack horse. Often he looked back, irritated that Twigs and Wiley, on his mule, rode slowly in the rear.

Finally Potluck reined up and waited for them. "What's keeping you? You know darn well the old man is waiting for us. He thinks you have the girl with you."

"Why would he think that?" Twigs asked.

"Potluck's right." Wiley offered. "No telling what Sid told him."

Twigs speculated. "Yeah, I guess he could have told his pa I was supposed to bring her along."

Potluck, who didn't know Sid had also messed his britches, repeated his warning. "Don't you ever say Sid was treed. The old man will skin you alive. And Sid will cut you down to shut you up for good." Potluck spat. "So you'd better get that old mule of yours to move a little faster."

The white mule put his ears back as if he had heard.

Potluck, glaring at the mule which hated him as much as he hated it, turned his mount and went back to leading the way with the pack horse.

Wiley and Twigs held back their grins until Potluck was out of earshot again.

Wiley covered his mouth and snorted as he forced his laugh into silence. To him and Twigs, what happened between Sid and Billy was a delight because of Sid's often loud bravado and bursting ego. Yes, Sid had been the fastest gun around—until now.

Twigs whispered to Wiley. "You'd better wipe that silly grin off your face before you get us both dead and buried."

Wiley choked on his laugh and wiped a tear from his eye. Then he leaned forward to stroke his mule on the neck. "Good boy."

And at the Callahan ranch late that same Tuesday afternoon, Blair sat on a porch bench with his brother Pike, shaded from the fading sun. They watched men working colts in a far corral by one of the three barns.

Pike squinted. "I don't see Sid around."

"Jody says he's in his room. Sick. "

"What about the girl?" Pike persisted.

"Seems Twigs is bringing her."

"Well, they're sure not here."

No, thought Blair, a little annoyed at the lack of information.

At that moment, Jody came out onto the porch, stretched, came over to them. "So where is she? It's getting awful late."

"How's your brother?" Blair asked.

"In his room, but he ain't sick. He's play-acting."

"I'll see about that," Blair said, standing up and favoring his right leg as he limped inside.

Jody grinned and sat down by Pike. "Sure be glad to see my bride again."

"You sure you know how to be a husband to a good woman?" Pike asked.

"Do you?"

Pike grinned. "Yeah, I had three wives."

"Where are they?"

"Worn out and long gone."

"You were married to all three at the same time?"

Pike chuckled. "Maybe the first was legal, but when she left, I found me one after the other."

Jody grinned and looked away, trying not to stare at Uncle Pike's twisted left hand.

In the house, Blair limped into Sid's room. The shades were drawn so it was dimly lit by a lamp on the dresser with the wick turned low. One wall held a rack of pistols, from Sid's first cap and ball to a series of new Colts.

Sid was fully dressed, sitting in a chair with a glass of whiskey. Blair had a lot of respect for his son and expected him to follow in his footsteps, but he didn't condone malingering. Sid looked sheepish.

Blair sat on a nearby chair. "What the devil is going on?"

It took a long while for Sid to answer, but he was busting to say it.

"Pa, I didn't have the guts to tell you."

"Tell me what?"

"Everybody's going to know when Twigs gets back."

"Is he bringing the girl?"

"Pa, I don't know on account of I left in a hurry." Sid swallowed hard. "You see, when we caught up to her, she was with Linstrom's wagon and some young gun hawk."

"And?"

"The kid, he came walking up like the devil himself." Sid downed his drink. "He beat me to the draw, Pa. Had me cold. I hadn't even cleared my holster. He was ready to shoot me dead."

"And?" Blair asked, leaning forward in disbelief. Sid had proven himself many times to be the fastest gun in the territory, if not the whole frontier. If there was a new gun in town, they might have to get rid of the interloper.

Sid choked on his drink, wiped his mouth, almost afraid to tell his father, but he knew he had better be the one to break the news. So he did.

"I messed my britches, dropped my gun belt, and come home."

It took awhile for Blair to swallow the story. "Why'd you take so long to tell me?"

"I was ashamed, Pa."

Blair felt his son's misery, but after years on the frontier in many a fight, he had seen men who'd suffered worse and would never be surprised at anything. "Where was Twigs?"

"The old man had a rifle on him. But he's no gun hand anyhow. But if Twigs tells anyone…"

"Don't worry about Twigs. He rides for the brand. And he knows what would happen if he doesn't keep his mouth shut."

"Old man Linstrom may tell it," Sid grumbled. "If anyone snickers behind my back…"

"You have my permission to shoot 'em."

Sid still worried. "Don't tell Jody or anyone else what I did."

"No, but pull yourself together. We need to catch up with that girl. Keep her mouth shut."

"She'd be too scared to say anything."

"I'll send for some hard cases, across the border. From Cinch. We've used 'em before. Get 'em here by morning."

"Jody's better off without her. I still got her bite marks on my hand."

"Ain't you ever figured why she run off?"

Sid frowned, shook his head, waited for the explanation.

Blair lowered his voice. "She must've been in the garden and heard us talking about killing her pa and why we done it."

Sid was startled. "She could get us hanged!"

Blair shook his head. "No one would believe her, but I still don't want her out there saying it either."

"If she heard us say it, then she'll just run away again." Sid stared into his empty glass. "Maybe we should just bury her someplace."

"No, she belongs to Jody." Blair pushed his hat back.

"Yeah, but does he even remember he killed that floozy?"

"No, he was too drunk at the time, so don't ever tell him."

"You spoil him, Pa."

Sid knew that because his mother had died in childbirth, his father saw Jody as a painful but loving reminder of her. Yet in all his life, Sid had never seen a tear in his father's eyes, except one time, when Blair had to shoot his beloved buckskin gelding.

Yes, his father spoiled Jody because the boy reminded him of the only woman he had ever loved. At the same time, Sid knew when his father was gone, he'd be running the ranch. Jody would just be a decoration.

Blair leaned forward. "So who was the gun hawk?"

"Just a kid. But I think his name is Billy Tyson."

"Never heard of him."

"I tell you, Pa, I didn't even see his hand move."

Blair mulled it over as Sid wiped his face with a handkerchief. Anyone faster than Sid had to be lightning-quick. So, no question, the gun hawk had to go.

"Why didn't he pull the trigger?" Blair asked.

"I don't know, but he said something about the Bonneville Ranch."

Blair hesitated. "Yeah? That was fifteen years ago. And you say he's just a kid?"

"He knew about it."

Blair grimaced and pushed his hat back. "I was told old man Bonneville had no kinfolk. And no one knows or even cares if we had to take out some squatters that moved in. Besides, we figured to just run 'em off, but they put up a devil of a fight. Not our fault. Just the same, there weren't no survivors, so I don't know how…"

"He said it real clear," Sid said. "And he was scary, Pa."

Blair made a face, then stood up. "Whoever he is, he won't get another chance for a fair fight. So get yourself together. Come morning, we're going after her."

"Maybe she's got on the stage at Rhyker's by now."

"Hardy's there to make sure that doesn't happen. Besides, I know the northbound's not due for another week, on account of they cut back. So there's no hurry."

"What about the old guy's wagon?"

"Rhyker's is as far north as Linstrom goes, and he's too smart to try to outrun us." Blair leaned over to put a hand on Sid's shoulder. "Come out on the porch with Pike."

"Pa, he's the only one I know who's meaner than you."

Blair grinned. "But he's not tougher. Just older."

"With a gun hawk on their side, they'll put up a fight for her, Pa. Won't look good for us if we kill old man Rhyker." Sid told him. "Let Jody go ahead and try to get her back."

"Not a bad idea. I'll send him with Twigs first thing tomorrow.

We'll head out the following day and camp at the springs, give him a chance that afternoon while we wait. But if he can't talk her back, we'll just go and take her."

"Why Twigs?"

"He's not trigger-happy and Jody likes him," Blair said. "We don't want trouble if we can avoid it."

"If she refuses to come back, they'll fort up."

"That station is right across from a big clump of ground covered with brush and rocks, and there's a gully behind it. We can wipe 'em out from there without losing a man."

"There's water?"

"A small spring, way back in the canyon, but if it's dry, Rhyker will let us get 'em to a trough. He's big on horses being cared for. And there's plenty of grass north of the knoll."

They both were deep in thought for a moment.

"The girl could get killed," Sid told him.

"That would solve our problem, wouldn't it?" Blair mused, then sobered.

They both paused to consider the idea, but Blair, ever wanting Jody to be happy, shrugged it off.

They got up and went outside to join Jody and Pike on the porch.

"Jody," said Blair as he sat on the next bench with Sid, "we figure you should leave tomorrow morning with Twigs. We'll follow a day later, and if you don't bring her back by the time we camp at the springs, we'll go after her the next day."

"Okay, Pa."

"No need to have an army," Pike said. "We can walk right over them."

"They hired a killer," Blair told him. "Kid named Billy Tyson."

"Never heard of him," Pike said, brushing it off.

"We'll have a few of our own, from Cinch." Blair added.

They sat a moment, all knowing that the men from Cinch were

hard to handle. They would have to make sure any fight was under control. At the same time, Blair was not about to risk too many of his ranch hands who were needed on the range. He also figured it would be easier to scare anyone at the station if he showed up with some seriously bad gunmen.

Now Sid walked to the edge of the porch and gestured.

"That's Potluck coming," Sid said.

They watched as Twigs, Wiley and Potluck rode up to the hitching rail.

Twigs held out Sid's gunbelt. Red-faced, Sid hesitated, then realized he had no choice. Reluctant, trying to strut and look unaffected, he came down the steps, walked over to Twigs, retrieved it, and went back up on the porch. No one dared ask why Twigs had it.

Potluck, seeing Sid's glare, knew to keep his mouth shut.

Blair stood and went to the porch rail. "Twigs, you and Jody head out tomorrow, get his wife from the station. We'll follow the next day, wait at the springs. "

"Maybe I should go along," Wiley said.

Knowing Wiley was a cool head, Blair nodded. In fact, Wiley was the only man alive Blair admired, because Wiley reminded him of Blair's beloved father who was just as much a frontiersman. Wiley didn't have a mean bone in his body, was sometimes a kick to be around, and knew stories to either make you laugh or scare you silly.

It was then that Pike stood up and joined his brother. He put his twisted left hand on the rail.

Twigs fought to keep a snarl from his face. *My God*, he thought, *it could be him.*

CHAPTER 4

While Blair made his plans at the Callahan Ranch late that same Tuesday afternoon, Rhyker's Station was busy with repairing the stage while the two passengers rested inside.

Standing near the smithy, with the coach close by, Rhyker watched as Chauncey worked iron while Mintz sanded some wood repairs. Marks supervised from the shade. Nothing they did seemed to stabilize the undercarriage.

"Doesn't look good," Mintz said.

Over at the corrals, Chipper was busy filling the water troughs. They all liked him. He had been a throw away by some passing wagon, skinny and half-starved. But as if overnight, he beefed up and had a ready laugh, loved everyone and loved to hear their stories. He had a big appetite for anything Nellie served, as if he had never eaten before.

Rhyker pushed his hat back and turned to look toward the station. He was proud of his work, had peace in his heart, loved his wife at first sight and treasured her. He was not looking for any trouble. Little did he know he would soon be in the middle of it.

Mintz followed his gaze at the station. "That Potts does nothing but complain, but the lady passenger puts him in his place just by glaring at him. Too bad she's married." Rhyker grinned. "What would an old geezer like you do with a pretty lady like her?"

Mintz started to reply but stopped.

They could see Linstrom's wagon coming from the south, the team straining with the slight rise in grade. A welcome sight. They all liked Red, played checkers with him and poker, chided him for fun, and missed him when he took off again.

"He's late," Rhyker said. "We were getting low on coffee."

Rhyker started back for the station.

Mintz was on his heels. "He's supposed to bring me a new gunbelt."

Curious, Marks left the smithy and followed them. Chauncey remained to continue the work as Chipper happily tried to help though he mostly just got in the way.

Nearing the station, Rhyker, Marks and Mintz could see that Linstrom had a young woman sitting to his left on the wagon seat. Between them, the border collie sat as if in charge. The girl was too young to be his wife, and he didn't have a daughter that old, so they were right curious.

And who was that young rider moving alongside to his right?

Marks squinted in the sunlight. "That's the Miller girl. I knew her pa, the sheriff, when I was a ranger up from Texas. Long before he was shot in the back."

"The same girl you said was marrying a Callahan?" Mintz asked.

"Yeah," Marks said. "And I smell trouble."

"Who's the rider?" Rhyker questioned.

"Some drifter, I suspect," Marks said as the wagon and rider came closer, then shook his head. "Maybe not. His holster's tied down. Could be a hired gun. A few of them head north from time to time."

"He looks like a kid."

"They all do, of late. But where's Hardy?"

"Out at the tack room where he bunks."

The two men didn't notice Hardy exiting the tack room behind them to observe the arrival.

As Red drove his wagon toward the station, Jocelyn stiffened and leaned forward on the wagon seat. She was afraid and tugged her jacket around her for comfort. Red could see she was agitated and spoke softly to her.

"Don't worry, darling."

"That's Mr. Marks. He knew my father. He was a Texas Ranger hunting someone up here back then. They got to be friends."

"Easy," Red cautioned.

She hugged herself and sat back. She worried, not that Marks knew her, but that everything around her was rising to a fever-pitch. It would be her fault if trouble followed her. *But*, she thought, *I'd rather die than go back.*

Next to the wagon, Billy rode in quiet thought. Yes, he was a fast gun. Years of practice, day and night, along with a natural skill, had brought him to Callahan country.

The truth had to be here, somewhere. He felt for Jocelyn, and any other woman under the threat of evil men. His nightmares would never end until he found his targets and doled out his own brand of justice.

Worse, in the middle of his silent desperation, Billy was feeling a surge of warmth and affection for Jocelyn, knowing it was dangerous to soften for any reason. But just being around her had a growing affect on his interest. *She can do a lot better than me*, he thought grimly. *She needs love and peace, and I don't know how to live like that.*

Red pulled up to Rhyker, Mintz and Marks. He grinned down at them. Jocelyn retreated from view as much as she could. She was ashamed of how she looked.

Billy backed his horse and rode behind the wagon, over to the hitching rail, left of the heavy vehicle.

Marks came around to help Jocelyn step down. Knowing who he was made it easier for her. He then led her forward, around the team of horses, and over to the front steps of the covered front porch. Rhyker came to take her in hand.

"Miss Miller, this is Joe Rhyker," Marks said. "He runs the station. And that old guy over there," gesturing toward Mintz, "that's the stage driver. Don't believe anything he says."

The dog stayed with Red, sitting on the bench next to him to watch her.

Red leaned forward. "Joe, this lady has no belongings."

"Not to worry, darling." Rhyker offered his arm and guided her up the steps. "My wife will take good care of you."

When she faltered, he put his arm around her and guided her up to the porch.

Red drove his wagon on a short distance and then around the north side of the station where there was an outside ramp to the back door of the storeroom. He pulled up as Chipper came to help unload the freight with Mintz and Chauncey assisting. Six crates of sweet smelling apples, greens and reds, were carefully moved inside near the door to the front room and close to the kitchen.

"You can drive it over to the south barn," Red said of his wagon, "and pack the wheels."

"Yes, sir," Chipper replied. "I'll take care of your team."

Red helped the border collie back up onto the wagon seat. "This is Kip. He lives in the wagon. I'll be around later to feed him."

Chipper stroked the dog, which immediately warmed to him.

"But don't spoil him," Red warned, trying to look serious.

Red turned over the lines to the happy youth.

Meanwhile Billy, still at the hitching rail facing the front porch in the sunlight, lifted the stirrup to loosen the cinch. He steeled himself as Marks came around, because he knew the man to be an ex-ranger as he had seen him in action more than once. They had never met, but Marks had the reputation of being fair and honest, let alone fast on the draw.

Just the same, Billy didn't want anyone watching him.

Marks stood behind the rail. "You're riding a Texas rig."

Billy nodded, silent.

"I'm Henry Marks. Ride shotgun on the stage."

"Billy Tyson."

Billy reluctantly took the outstretched hand, then withdrew.

"I spent some years in Texas as a ranger. Never met any Tysons."

Billy took his concertina from the saddle horn and held it in his left hand.

"Heading north?" Marks persisted.

Billy turned, made sure no one else could hear. "I'm here to kill a few men, but I don't know who they are. Not yet."

Startled, Marks took a minute to recover. "So why did you tell me that?"

"Saves time. And a lot of questions."

Marks suddenly grinned, finding he liked the young gunman. "Okay, but I wouldn't spread that around. And it's for sure I won't."

"I know."

Marks hesitated. "Why is that?"

"I knew about you when I was in Texas."

Marks shrugged at the obvious compliment, then relaxed.

They walked around the rail and over to the steps. They climbed up to find Jocelyn sitting on a bench with Rhyker standing helpless nearby. She was pale, shivering, and visibly ashamed of her ratty appearance, not having been able to contain her tangled hair nor the pain she had suffered.

"She won't go inside," Rhyker said.

Billy walked over and offered his hand. She looked up to see the man who had saved her from Sid, a young daring man she felt great attraction for, but a man who was likely a hired gun. She hesitated, then took Billy's hand. He drew her to her feet, and she took his arm. He led her over to the door.

"See?" Marks grinned at Rhyker. "You're just too old."

"Speak for yourself," Rhyker said.

Inside the station, there was no sign of Potts. Eloise and Nellie were at a table having coffee. Nellie stood and came forward to greet Jocelyn as Billy led her inside, followed by Rhyker and Marks.

Jocelyn saw concern in both women. She felt she would be safe with them.

Nellie needed no prompting. She could see the girl was miserable.

"Nellie," Rhyker said, "this is Miss Miller. She needs help."

Immediately, Nellie took charge and Eloise quickly stood. The two women led Jocelyn to the hallway and out of sight of the others.

Billy stood looking lost. He still carried his concertina.

Rhyker quickly took over. "Have a seat. I'll bring some coffee."

As Billy and Marks sat down at the table, Red and Mintz came inside and sat with them. Red's dog, fed and watered, had stayed in the wagon to protect it, always making it a duty. At the same time, Red knew for sure that Chipper was in there with Kip, having a lively one-sided conversation.

Rhyker had disappeared into the kitchen. Red introduced Billy to the stage driver, who shook hands and now stared toward the kitchen.

"It's chow time," Mintz grumbled.

Red set out a shipping list for Rhyker, who came back from the kitchen with a tray of mugs and the pot. He poured hot coffee for everyone, then sat down.

Rhyker studied the list. "Apples!"

"My wife sent 'em," Red responded, "and I'm not leaving till I get some apple pie."

"I can taste it now," Rhyker said. "And it won't last long."

"They aren't full-ripe, but I can wait," Red added, moistening his lips. "When's the northbound due?"

"Another week. They cut back on the runs, even though I've told them the Mescaleros never come this way. You know something I don't?"

Red spoke low. "That girl in there is Jocelyn Miller, but she just married up with Jody Callahan a little over a week ago."

Marks didn't like what he heard, because he knew of the Callahans. Billy was silent, wanting to hear every new word about the clan.

"So why is she here?" Rhyker asked softly.

"She said she was in the garden that night, while the reception was going on at the ranch, and she overheard Sid and old man Callahan saying how her father was shot because he was going to arrest Jody for killing a saloon girl."

Marks immediately reacted. "She say who shot him?"

"She figured they were saying it was Sid," Red continued, "but nothing was for sure. Anyhow, she stole a horse and lit out that same night, crossed to the mountains in hopes they wouldn't find her. The horse run off. And then she comes down on the road, all torn up, just ahead of us. Sid was right behind her. And some fellow named Twigs following."

"Brave girl," Mintz said.

Billy sipped his coffee, silent as Red continued. He could see again the ragged, bleeding young woman, staggering on the road as Sid tried to carry her away.

Red continued. "So when Sid got down and tried to beat on her, Billy, here, he got over there and told him to lay off. Sid figures himself the fastest gun around, so he goes to draw on him, and his

Colt's half out of his holster, but Billy had already pulled his and was aiming right at him."

Rhyker grinned. "Wish I coulda seen that."

Marks listened intently, assessing further this young man from Texas. Anyone that fast was to be reckoned with, let alone likely to stir up a lot of trouble.

Billy looked embarrassed, stared into his coffee.

Red had to chuckle. "Ole Sid let his pistol drop back in his holster. He kept staring at Billy's Colt, figuring he was about to die. So he messed his britches. Real bad. Had a funny look on his face."

Rhyker choked on his coffee. Mintz burst out in a grin.

"Billy just stood there, aiming," Red said, "but he made ole Sid drop his gunbelt and head for home."

Billy suddenly took up his concertina, then stopped before playing it. No one knew the turmoil that dwelled in him or why he was after a reckoning.

"Maybe no one's heard of you, Billy," Marks said, "but the Callahans sure have by now."

Billy fondled his musical instrument and fought back painful memories. He had to admit he enjoyed facing down Sid Callahan. If that clan turned out to be Billy's target, he was on his way to rattling their cage until the truth was known.

"They'll be coming after her," Red warned.

Chipper came inside and over to the table. "That fellow Hardy, he took off. Riding south like a bat out of heck."

"How's my dog?" Red asked of him. Chipper just grinned.

Then the youth went outside and back to the smith to finish helping Chauncey.

"Hardy?" Red asked after a moment.

"Hired gun, works for the Callahans," Rhyker said. "Been hanging around near on a week. I guess he was waiting for her to show up. Now he figures there's too many of us, so he's headed for home to get help."

Red made a face. "We think it's already on its way. But I could take her north in my wagon."

"They'll just track you down," Rhyker said. "And you'd be all by your lonesome out there. Besides, this is your turn around point."

"Yeah," Red finally agreed. "But their ranch is all heck and gone south of here, so I figure you got maybe a couple days before they show up."

Billy suddenly stood, nodded to them, and went outside to be alone with his thoughts. They could soon hear his concertina on the porch as he played a soft ballad.

Marks leaned forward. "What do you know about that kid?"

Red smiled. "All I know is, he's probably the fastest draw west of the Mississippi. And what's more, I don't figure Billy's afraid of anything, except maybe that girl." He sobered. "But he's carrying some kind of hate and looks ready to explode."

Marks silently agreed.

They were pretty hungry, but it was nearly an hour before Nellie returned. There was no sign of Eloise or Jocelyn. Nellie went in the kitchen to start supper. Chipper and Chauncey came in and found seats at the next table.

A grumpy Potts entered and sat by himself.

"That one acts like he's got something up his rear end," Mintz whispered.

That night in Eloise's room, which had two beds and a shuttered window, Eloise was making her guest as comfortable as she could. Jocelyn wore a flannel night gown given to her by Nellie. On a rack, several print gingham dresses, including one with blue checks and another green, were hanging. Empty trays of food were on the center table.

"That bath felt so good," Jocelyn said. "You and Nellie have been so nice."

"With what you've been through?" Eloise replied. "But there may be trouble, so tell me, can you fire a weapon?"

"Yes, my father was a sheriff and taught me."

"If there's a fight, will you be able to join in?"

"Not to save myself from being taken away," Jocelyn said. "But to save you or Nellie, or someone else, yes, I could pull the trigger. But I don't know if I could live with hurting anyone. Especially the man I married."

"Don't take your vows so seriously. You never would have said yes if you'd known the truth."

"But I can't let anyone get hurt because of me," Jocelyn said. "I'd have to go back before I let that happen."

"No one's going to let you do that," Eloise said. "I'd lock you in your room first."

"You're sweet," Jocelyn said, touched. "But no one's going to die because of me. Maybe I can get away from here before they come."

"They'd just track you down," Eloise said. "You're safer here."

"But none of you are."

Eloise saw the young woman's stress rising, so she changed the subject. They began to talk about clothes. Jocelyn enjoyed the attention, having grown up without a mother and missing the closeness of caring women.

Eloise teased her. "And what about you and that young cowboy out there? I see how you look at him."

"Billy? He saved me from Sid, but that's all. He's not interested."

Eloise laughed softly. "When I was a young girl, there was this wild cowboy named Hank working on my father's ranch. He wanted nothing to do with women. I couldn't even get him to dance with me."

"So what did you do?"

70

"Come the Fourth of July, there was a rifle shooting contest, and all the cowboys and men in town were trying for this brand new Winchester Repeater."

Jocelyn leaned forward. "And?"

"I won, hands down."

Jocelyn smiled happily. "And then?"

"Well, all of a sudden, I wasn't just a girl. Maybe they could out-ride and out-rope me, but I was always flashing that rifle."

"And then what happened?"

"Hank and some others were going hunting for a wild boar that had killed a man. I wanted to go, and Hank said if I went along, he wasn't going."

"And then?"

"I started punching him. We got in a struggle, and we rolled off the bank and down into the Rio Grande. We hit the water in a clinch, and we never let go. Not for twenty-five years and nine kids."

"Where is he now?"

"Oh, he's running the ranch, on account of my father married a young widow and took off for California."

They had a good laugh. Jocelyn's spirits were high, at least for the moment.

*   *   *   *   *

Early Wednesday morning at the station, the empty freight wagon rested next to the south barn, having now had its wheels greased. The dog sat on the wagon seat, always in charge.

Over at the smithy, Chauncey was still trying to repair the stage. He had help from Mintz, the driver.

Chauncey grumbled. "Could use some coffee about now."

"That Nellie sure can cook," Mintz said. "Too bad Rhyker found her first."

71

"Took a lot of horses to get her." Chauncey said. "I don't figure you even have a pot to…"

"Oh, yeah?" Mintz countered, then laughed.

The men chuckled, turned to their work.

They had propped up the coach and dismantled the rear axle, which was bent as bad as the front one. Chauncey stared at it, scratched his head. Mintz, looked toward the station. Smoke came from the station chimney.

"Breakfast," Mintz said.

They headed for the station. Chipper, out in the corral, jumped the fence to follow.

Inside the station that same morning, Peter Potts, the stuffy Bostonian, sat alone. No one chose to sit with him. Chauncey and Chipper sat at another table.

Rhyker, Red Linstrom, Billy Tyson, Mintz and Marks sat by themselves, with one empty chair between Billy and Red. They could smell breakfast from the kitchen.

All had been served coffee by Rhyker, himself.

Billy sat quiet, evaluating these men. He liked everyone of them, but not Potts, who was out of earshot. Billy had spent a lot of years alone on the trail with no results, but now he felt it would be a lot easier with friends like these. They were older and had seen more of life. Not one of them acted judgmental.

"You know," Mintz said to Rhyker, "if you'd help your wife, we'd be eating by now."

"She don't want anybody messing around in her kitchen," Red offered. "And Joe here, he's scared silly of her."

Joe Rhyker and the others laughed. "I just know better," Rhyker said.

From the hallway to the left, Eloise appeared and coaxed Jocelyn to follow.

Now bathed, her flaxen hair fluffy on her shoulders, wearing a blue dress with a white collar, Jocelyn looked lovely.

Billy stared in awe and got to his feet as the others at his table stood. *My God*, he thought, *she's so beautiful. If I ever had a free life, maybe, but I'm kidding myself. I'd never have a chance with her.*

Eloise guided her to the empty chair between Billy and Red. Jocelyn resisted, wanting to stay with her.

"No, honey," Eloise said, "I have to sit with Mr. Potts, because no one else will."

"That can't be any fun," Rhyker said.

"Oh, but it is," Eloise answered. "I get to yank his chain now and then."

The men all grinned at her as she turned to join Potts.

Shyly, Jocelyn gathered her skirts around her and sat down between Billy and Red. When the men all sat down around her, Billy looked like he wanted to skedaddle.

"Miss Miller, you look grand," Red offered.

Jocelyn felt welcome, something she had never experienced at the Callahan Ranch. These men made her feel pretty and comfortable. Even Billy had cast an admiring glance, which had warmed her heart.

Nellie came with a pot of coffee and a cup for Jocelyn. Ignoring their hungry looks, Nellie returned to the kitchen.

No one at the station was aware that on that same Wednesday night, Twigs, Wiley and Jody were camped at Seven Springs a long way down the road.

Jody sat brooding by the campfire. He was so in love with the image of his bride. He had hardly ever talked with her about life, her father, her work as a schoolteacher, or books she had read. He had never asked of her dreams and aspirations. All he wanted was to have a beautiful girl all to himself. It had also made him feel more important than his overbearing brother. He had never expected to be rejected without knowing why.

Wiley and Twigs, both feeling sorry for Jody, walked off and out of earshot.

"That kid doesn't know what day it is," Wiley remarked.

"No, and he's not much of a threat. But I sure wouldn't turn my back on Sid."

"What about the old man?" Twigs asked.

"Blair Callahan thinks he's king. He figures everything he does is what he's destined to do. But he talks straight, doesn't try to fool anyone. He's just what he seems, and if you get on his bad side, look out. He'll shoot you down and go have breakfast."

Twigs hesitated. He could see that Wiley respected Blair, warts and all, but wasn't fooled by the tyrant. "So why'd you go to work for him?"

"So I could get paid and take it easy. He needed a tracker, so I find him mountain lions, wild boars and rustlers. He doesn't ask anything else of me." Wiley felt a pang. "Besides, when I lost my Cheyenne wife up in the Rockies, I was already feeling the cold in my bones, so I came south."

Twigs yawned. "Well, you sure messed up with the girl. You rode right over the signs where she was headed for the mountains and then you led him west on the cattle trail."

"You saw her, right? You ever want a Callahan to get his hands on her?"

Twigs shook his head, feeling pain for any woman in trouble.

Wiley paused to look up at the night sky and twinkling stars. "Might rain in a day or so."

"Beats me how you can smell it coming. Have you ever been wrong?"

"Once, maybe. When it hailed instead."

Twigs grinned. He liked Wiley so much, he wanted Billy to

meet him. The aging mountain man was just what he seemed. A good old fellow who didn't have an ax to grind.

"You always ride a mule?" Twigs asked.

"Yeah, they keep their head when all goes wrong. And he rattles ole Potluck. Gives me a chuckle now and then."

"What is it with Potluck?"

"Not much. He's just a boot-licker. Always making sure he looks good to Blair."

They walked back to the fire where Jody sat resting against his saddle, covered with a blanket and staring into the fire.

Wiley sat down with his harmonica and played soft music for a long while, but stopped when he noticed Jody lay asleep.

* * * * *

Late Thursday morning, the coach was still being repaired. Chauncey, Chipper and Mintz had been working for hours but the work was not done. Every time they tried to set it upright and straight, the wood cracked and metal wouldn't hold.

Chauncey shook his head. "Those must have been pretty big rocks."

"We came around the bend on our way down and there they was. Not so big, just so many stacked so high you couldn't miss. Must have been a rock slide."

"Got no idea when we will get this right."

"I don't mind," Mintz said. "Nellie's one heck of a cook. And it's about time for the noon meal."

They started toward the station. Chauncey limped along with him.

"But dang it, I haven't seen any apple pies yet," Mintz complained.

Chauncey grinned. "You leave before she cooks 'em, I'll make sure to take a few bites for you."

"You're all heart."

"Besides, if you don't get that Potts out of here pretty soon, she'll have your hide."After the noon meal, they went back to the smithy to work on the coach.

That afternoon, the others—even Potts—ventured onto the front porch to sit in the shade.

Nellie, Eloise and Jocelyn sat on one of the benches near the front door with Jocelyn in the center. Potts sat alone to the far left. Marks, Rhyker and Red sat with Billy on the other side of the door.

Billy was coaxed into playing music on his concertina. He played soft ballads while everyone listened with appreciation. No one sang, but when Jocelyn leaned forward to look at Billy, the other women glanced knowingly at each other.

Jocelyn was obviously in love, but she was emotionally broken and didn't know herself for sure. She'd seen other young gunfighters when her father rousted them. Yet this one was her hero. She could still feel his arms around her when he lifted her to the wagon, something she would never forget.

Billy, however much he admired her, had no emotions to share. Wrapped in a storm of revenge, his only comfort was his concertina. He played "Barbara Allen," "I gave My Love a Cherry," and his favorite, "Red River Valley," but he didn't sing, nor did anyone else.

The music drifted like a soft breeze, making the others sleepy.

Suddenly, Billy was alert. He stopped playing and set aside the instrument. He stood and came forward to the porch rail.

"Riders coming," he said.

Red, Marks and Rhyker stood up and joined Billy, standing to his left.

Red squinted in the sun. "I see that fellow Twigs."

Rhyker leaned forward. "And Wiley, he's the old time buffalo hunter, works for the Callahans as a kind of retirement. Can't miss him. But who's the one on the pinto?"

Red gestured. "It's Jody Callahan."

When Jocelyn started to rise to escape, Nellie and Eloise stopped her.

"Don't you worry," Nellie said. "We won't let him take you."

"We have to set him straight," Eloise said, "and if he doesn't see you, he'll think you're being held against your will."

Wiley and Jody reined up a short distance to the south.

Twigs came riding alone and reined up facing the porch.

Rhyker, Red and Marks were firm at the porch rail. Billy stood nearby.

Twigs obviously recognized Marks. He saluted the former ranger. Marks nodded and tipped his hat.

Billy and Twigs exchanged silent glances.

Back with the other women on the bench, Jocelyn shivered.

Twigs cleared his throat. "I've been sent to make way for Jody to see his wife."

"What for?" Rhyker asked.

"He wants her back."

Red grimaced. "She's right sure her father was murdered by the Callahans. Why in the devil would she want to see him?"

Twigs leaned on the horn. "Jody says he got no idea why she ran off. He figures she owes him an explanation."

Red pushed his hat back. "She won't see him alone. We'll bring her up to the porch rail, and that's all."

Now Billy was standing right next to Red with Marks and Rhyker to their left.

"Nobody's touching her, not ever," Billy said.

Twigs straightened in the saddle. "Billy, you got to know. Sid Callahan is planning to hang you."

Billy nodded. "I figured as much."

Twigs shifted his weight. "They'll have a dozen or more gun hands with them. A day behind us. They'll be camped at Seven Springs by tonight. If Jody doesn't bring her back now, they'll show up here tomorrow, sometime in the afternoon, for sure."

Rhyker put his hand on the porch rail. "You tell Jody Callahan to ride up here alone. And stay in the saddle."

Twigs spoke directly to Billy. "I finally met Pike Callahan. Blair's older brother and a lot meaner. Except he has a crippled left hand. And I know for a fact, Pike never did no ranch work, so it's not from a dally. But I don't know if he was in the War."

Billy put his hand on his holster. He looked ready to jump the rail as his tortured thoughts reeled. *From getting it caught in a windless? Throwing a ten-year-old down a dry well? Burning and killing?*

Marks didn't miss Billy's reaction. He saw a young gunman suddenly in a rage.

Rhyker, Red and Mintz had no idea why Pike mattered.

Twigs tugged on his hat brim. There was a long silence. Billy gripped the rail with his left hand. Inside he was seething, his hunger for justice like fire in his belly. He and Twigs exchanged even more knowing glances.

At length, Twigs turned and rode slowly south toward Jody and Wiley.

Rhyker turned to Billy. "Was that a friend of yours?"

Billy shrugged and didn't answer.

Back by the bench in the shade of the porch roof, Jocelyn stood up between Nellie and Eloise, who supported her. Red went to take her arm and lead her forward. She shivered in dread. At the rail, Red kept his left arm around her. Rhyker and Marks were to their left as Billy came forward to Red's other side at the porch rail, waiting. Jody rode forward alone.

In the safety of the four men who circled her, Jocelyn tried to be brave. She had always had some fear of Blair and Sid, for the kind of men they were. She had accepted Jody as he was, foolish and happy, but that had changed. Now she was also afraid of him.

Jody rode up unarmed and reined to a halt by the rail. He removed his hat, the sun shining on his dark, greasy hair. "Honey, darling," he pleaded to Jocelyn, "won't you come home with me?"

Jocelyn shook her head and shivered in the circle of Red's arm. "No."

"Honey," Jody persisted. "You don't want my pa to come riding up here tomorrow and kill everybody, do you?"

Red hugged her to his side. "Young fellow, you just forget about her and tell your pa the same."

"But I love her."

"That why you killed a saloon woman?" Red asked.

Jody went blank. "What?"

"And why this girl's pa was shot down by your brother so you wouldn't be arrested and hanged?"

Jody looked dumbfounded. "*What?*"

"She'll be getting the marriage annulled," Red informed him. "And we'll be helping her do just that."

Jody obviously didn't remember what had happened while he was drunk, and he had no clear understanding of why her father was shot. He was confused, a little shaken. Yet all he wanted was his wife, and he began to boil.

"She don't come with me, you're all going to die."

Potts stood up and waved to Jody. "I'm no part of this."

Jody ignored Potts and continued to glare at the men.

Jocelyn sobbed, pressed her face to Red's shoulder. Just looking at Jody was too painful, knowing what she knew, and never wanting him to touch her again.

"We'll be here. Waiting," Red told Jody.

Jody looked over at the coach repair, which had stopped while Chauncey and Chipper paused to watch the station. Now he looked at the dangerous Billy and the resolute Linstrom. He gazed longingly up at Jocelyn as she turned away with the women claiming her and leading her back inside. He gave a last, nasty look at Billy.

"Nobody's getting out of here until I get my wife back."

Then Jody turned his horse and rode south at a sudden lope. He headed back to where Wiley and Twigs were waiting. He would not ask them about the story he had been told, choosing instead to wait for his father. The three of them would return to the springs by nightfall, where Blair's army should also be making camp.

Back at the station, standing on the porch, Billy looked across the road at the high ground. "That's their only cover?"

"Yeah, if we can keep them wrapped up there." Rhyker said. "The knoll was cut back for the road. Pretty rocky on top. There's a gully to the back of it and up a canyon. And a spring but it's probably dry. Then the hills go up pretty steep behind it."

"A natural fort," Marks commented. "But we have to keep them from crossing over and getting behind us."

"I can take care of that," Mintz said. "From the smithy."

"We'll get you some rifles and another shotgun," Rhyker said. "But don't get in the fight if it happens. You'd be too lonely out there. Just don't let 'em cross over."

Mintz started to leave, then paused. "You might tell your missus I'd sure like to see some of that apple pie."

Rhyker grinned. "You'll know when she's baking. You'll smell the spices a mile away."

Mintz smacked his lips and grinned. He went down the steps

and back to helping with the stage repair, leaving Marks, Red, Rhyker and Billy on the porch.

Potts came a few steps forward. "Mr. Rhyker, you can't possibly want us all to die just to keep a man's wife from him? And protect some gunfighter?"

Rhyker just waved him away.

Fretting, Potts retreated back inside where the women had already gone.

"We'd better be prepared," Billy said.

"What are you thinking?" Rhyker asked.

Billy studied the high ground across the stage road to the east. "You got any dynamite around here?"

Rhyker, startled, nodded. "Yeah, maybe three left from when they blasted the road through here. Buried behind the barn, but it may well be sweating by now. Could be real dangerous."

Marks adjusted his hat, looked at Billy. "You know dynamite?"

"What's there to know?" Billy asked.

"Geez, Billy," Red told him, "if it's wet, that's nitro."

Rhyker gestured. "Billy and I will take a look. No use everyone getting blown up."

"But I know more about it," Red persisted. "For one thing, if you're thinking of planting it on that rise, one shot in a stick could trigger the rest of 'em if you don't do it right."

"Then we have to be smart about it," Billy said.

Rhyker grinned, shook his head and looked at Red. "If you know so much, you help Billy dig it up. Chauncey will show you where."

Red made a face. "What are you going to do?"

"I'm going inside," Rhyker said. "My wife will give me the biggest empty tin cans she's got. And oil cloth from the crates. And some rawhide strings."

Marks stood at the porch rail and gazed south. "I'll stand watch."

CHAPTER 5

Outside that Thursday afternoon at Rhyker's Station, Mintz, Red Linstrom and Billy Tyson walked over to the smithy where Chauncey and Chipper worked with some red-hot iron bars. Mintz had filled them in on the coming threat.

"We need to find the dynamite," Red added.

A nervous Chauncey then took up a shovel and led Billy and Red behind the barn which opened into the first corral where horses were sunning themselves.

"Next to that post," Chauncey said, nodding to a marker at the barn's back wall, "but it could blow up on you, so give me time to move the horses to the next corral."

"I'll help," Billy said.

Red stood back with the shovel and waited. He wiped his brow. Yes, he knew dynamite, and that was why he was sweating more than the sticks might be.

At the same time, inside the station, Potts and Eloise sat at a table with coffee near a front window. Jocelyn was in her room. No one else was present in the front room.

Potts held his cup in both hands. "How can you possibly be so calm about all this?"

"It's easy," Eloise replied. "Just sit through a hurricane or tornado, or try to survive a flood. Or stampede. Or bandits. Maybe Comanches. We learn how to deal with anything in Texas."

"I hear it's an ugly place."

"Be glad I'm unarmed," she said, pointedly.

"Well, isn't it?"

"No, and it's so big, you could put four or five other states inside of it. Arizona desert. New Mexico cliffs. Kentucky hills. Montana grassland. And fish off the coastline for miles. Not to mention the Rio Grande and Big Bend Country. Texas has everything."

"It'll never have me."

"Thank God for that." She smiled but her tone was sharp.

Potts was about to snap at her but stopped suddenly.

Rhyker sped in the front door and went to join Nellie in the kitchen. Right after, there was clanging and rattling of metal.

Potts was perplexed. When Nellie brought more coffee, he questioned her.

"What's going on?" he demanded.

"Nothing you need to know," Nellie snapped.

"I have my rights!"

For a long moment, Nellie held the pot of hot coffee close to his chest and right over his lap. She let it wobble in her grip. He turned pale. Any second he could get a hot shower in a very delicate spot.

After a moment, seeing he was about to whimper, Nellie took the pot and turned away. Potts wiped his face with his handkerchief.

When Nellie went back into the kitchen, Potts regained his posture and made a fuss. "Don't they know my family owns half of Boston?"

Eloise just smiled but was a little disappointed the coffee pot hadn't leaked on him.

Rhyker came out of the kitchen with a gunny sack full of various size cans, rawhide strings, and some oil skins. He paused as Potts waved at him. Rhyker moved closer.

"This is the worst place I've ever been," Potts said. "I may just report you."

Rhyker grunted while trying to keep a straight face. "If you don't like our station, you'll love the next one south of here, where you camp in a canyon by the springs. You'll sleep in the coach or on the ground, less you're afraid of snakes."

Potts looked pained. "What?"

"And," Rhyker gleefully continued, "the nearest necessary is a tree."

Potts stared at him. "*What?*"

Eloise tried not to laugh. "It's my favorite spot."

Potts could barely contain himself. "That's outrageous! Why wasn't I told?"

Rhyker grunted. "If you don't like it out West, you may want to go back home."

"I have business in El Paso."

Rhyker needed his customers, and Potts was one, but the man was pushing his luck.

"We're all pretty good shots out here," Rhyker said to him, "but what we really need is a sharpshooter, on account of the first shot has to be a bulls-eye. How about you?"

"I don't use firearms," Potts snapped.

"Too bad," Rhyker said, tongue in cheek. "I was counting on you to save us."

Eloise held up her hand. "Mr. Rhyker, I never miss. In fact, I won every rifle shoot on the Fourth for seven years down in Texas."

Potts sneered. "Then you lost?"

She laughed. "No, they were tired of my winning and decided to make it for men only. Said a woman might get hurt."

"Good, so we'll count on you," Rhyker said to her with a grin, then headed outside.

"The line's going to hear about this," Potts grumbled.

"You're not helping the situation," Eloise said. "In fact, all you do is whine."

"What gives you the right to judge a man like me? You're just a woman."

"I'm not the only woman here." She smiled and sipped her coffee. "You notice how Mrs. Rhyker admires your hair?"

"What?"

"Make a good scalp to hang over her back door."

"She's just a squaw."

"So you just don't like women." She sipped her coffee. "You have a wife at home?"

Potts had a look of disgust. "No. Wives spend too much money. And they're always wanting something. And when you're gone, they spend every penny you worked hard to get."

Potts finally simmered down, but he soon stood up and went to his room.

Eloise giggled and leaned back, enjoying her coffee.

Nellie came out with her own cup and sat down. "I was waiting for him to leave."

"He's afraid of you."

"He should be," Nellie said with a chuckle.

Out behind the barn in the fading afternoon sun, Red Linstrom uncovered the wooden box which he had dug up from the ground. With great anxiety and sweat on his brow, he brought it out of the hole and bent over to carefully open it. Nothing exploded.

Finally, he knelt to look at the three. "Stand back, Billy," he warned.

Billy moved but stayed where he could see.

Rhyker came with the cans and stood back with Billy. "I have the longest cans I could find. And some strings. And oilskin."

"Okay," Red told them when he stood up. "It's sweating but I think we can move it in cans. We need a bucket of water to float them until we can get 'em where we want 'em."

"The knoll is maybe forty feet wide," Rhyker said. "How you gonna do it?"

"We can stagger them near the top," Red replied. "They'll blow with the line of least resistance, which is up. Give a dirt shower right off, knock a few of them down on their rumps. But no need unless they fire on us first."

Rhyker wiped the sweat from his brow. "When we refuse to give up the girl, they'll fire on us, all right, but just to scare us. If we stand our ground and fight back, they'll lay into us so fast, we may not be able to hold 'em off. We'll have to blow a stick."

"So who's gonna take the first shot at one?" Red quizzed.

"We're lucky to have a sharpshooter on hand," Rhyker said.

"You mean Billy?" Red suggested.

"No, the lady passenger. She won a heap of rifle shoots in Texas."

"Well, I'll be," Red remarked as he took one of the cans.

*   *   *   *   *

That same Thursday as night fell, Jody, Wiley and Twigs were riding south away from the station. They soon neared the Seven Springs campground east of the stage road where the springs and pond aided all travelers. It faced a canyon lined with cottonwoods and birch. The hills rose sharply behind it.

The rising moon added light to the stars.

Jody had been silent all the way. Rhyker's words burned in his confused mind. He did not believe any of it was true, but he wasn't going to tell anyone but his father.

As they arrived, they found Blair, Sid, Pike and some twenty gun hands, including Hardy and Potluck, already camped with a hot fire shooting up red and yellow flames. Two pack mules, bare of their load, stood off near the road. The horses were hobbled, haltered, and grazed nearby.

Jody did not have his bride with him, and he looked so down, no one spoke of it, but he did meet his father's gaze and shook his head. They ate supper around the campfire with Jody brooding in silence.

When most of the men were asleep in their bedrolls, Jody stood and led his father aside, out of earshot. The night was chilly with a lone coyote howling off in the distance.

They stood near the trees under the pale light of the stars and moon. Blair doted on his son, even when he knew the boy was soft, easy, self-indulgent, and downright useless on the ranch. He just didn't admit to son's failings. His son could do no wrong.

It was obvious that Jocelyn had either refused to come with Jody or was not allowed, for which someone would pay.

"Did you see her?" Blair asked.

"Yeah, but she said no and refused to come off the porch, so they took her away."

"They?"

"The women took her inside, but that Red Linstrom, he said she was not going back with me. He said I killed a woman?"

Jody's anguished whine hung in the air for a long moment.

Blair hesitated. "Well, son, if that's true, it was probably an accident. They said you were drunk and pushed Posey down the staircase."

"Posey?" Jody queried. "The skinny one? She's dead?"

"The sheriff was coming to arrest you, so Sid shot him down, from an alley."

"What?" Joey stammered in dismay. "My wife's father?"

"We didn't want you to hang."

"Pa, I don't remember any of it."

"Just as well."

"Does my wife know?"

"She found out that night at the reception. And that's why she ran away."

"She must hate me."

"Women get over things, Jody, and she knows you don't have a mean bone in your body. We'll get her back home, and sooner or later, she'll be okay with you, once you bed her down. And you'll buy her lots of pretties. A fancy carriage. Maybe take her on a nice trip somewhere."

"What if we can't get her back?"

"Son, don't worry. I got an extra ten gun hands hired out of Cinch. And Hardy. And a few of our own. No matter what happens, we're covered."

As Joey and his father talked away from camp, Twigs stood guard further up the road. He could not hear what they were saying, but he could guess. At the station, it had been obvious that Jody didn't remember doing anything wrong.

He now saw that Sid had joined his father and brother. The Callahans continued to talk in low voices.

After a time, Pike got up and walked over to them as Twigs watched and gritted his teeth at the sight of Pike's crippled left hand. *It had to be them, but we got no proof.* Twigs thought to himself with painful recollection. *And now I got to hold Billy down so he stays alive.*

Memories plagued Twigs, who had been only seventeen when he saw the remains of the death and destruction at the Bonneville Ranch. Helping with the burials could never be forgotten. He knew Billy had double the agony, having lived through it. For years, Billy had practiced every day with his fast draw. Twigs had been the searcher, finding out all he could about who might have led the raid. Now they had pretty much ruled out everyone but the Callahans.

Wiley came over to Twigs, stood with him and waved toward the camp. "We got to do something about this. Some of these characters are cold-blooded killers. It could get out of hand."

"Yeah, I know." Twigs reflected. "Was Pike in the Civil War? I mean, he's got a crippled hand. And he never did no ranch work."

"None of 'em was in the War," Wiley said. "They were too busy making money off both sides with beef and horses."

"Do you know how Pike got hurt?"

"No, I don't and I ain't never gonna ask." Wiley shook his head. "He's a mean son of a gun. Don't ever cross him. I seen him bash a man's head in with a crowbar."

Wiley didn't ask why Twigs wanted to know, but he figured it was a reason that Wiley didn't want to hear. He liked things peaceable. With creaking joints and sleepless nights, Wiley just wanted to live as long as he could in the land he loved.

Twigs just stood quiet until Wiley spoke again.

"The old man wants me to ride ahead and circle around, camp behind the station aways back, to keep anyone from sneaking her out that way. He knows I got no interest in killing, but he figures I can scare the daylights of 'em with my Sharps."

"It's a boomer, all right," Twigs agreed. "But I give you just long enough to smell breakfast coming from the kitchen the next morning."

Wiley smacked his lips. "Yeah, Mrs. Rhyker makes the best flapjacks in the whole country."

*   *   *   *   *

Friday morning, just before noon, Red Linstrom and Billy Tyson had already dug holes for the three sticks of dynamite, which were in shiny tin cans and wrapped in oil skins. The explosives were spread along and nearly two feet from the top of the brushy, rocky-top knoll. The cans were set to be easily seen from the station but not from riders who would have no reason to look.

Now Red and Billy retreated to the front porch where freight was stacked up on both sides, but away from the rail. They joined Rhyker, Eloise and Marks up by the rails in the late morning sun. They could see Mintz, Chauncey and Chipper over at the smithy, still trying to rebuild the coach's undercarriage.

Billy wanted action, but he didn't want his friends hurt.

Eloise put her hand on the rail, shaded her eyes and stared at the rise. "I see the cans. It's an easy shot."

"Maybe it won't be necessary," Rhyker said. "Maybe they'll back off."

Red made a face. "But if not, we can hope the sticks blow the top off and anyone above or behind it. There are three, so start in the middle. You'll give 'em a heck of a scare and maybe stop them from attacking the station. If you don't miss."

"I don't miss," she said. "Not if the rifle is properly sighted."

"You'll have my new Winchester, and it's got a deadly aim," Red answered. "So don't worry."

"Are you sure they'll hide back there?" she asked, staring at the knoll.

"Yeah, they'll want the cover while they try to intimidate us." Red told her.

"And if I hit one and nothing happens?"

"Unlikely," Red replied. "They were run with nitro, but if you have to, just keep firing at them."

Eloise stared a long while at the three half-buried cans. Finally she turned and went back inside.

Red fussed. "She's a nice lady, but they spot her, she could be a target. Don't want her hurt."

Rhyker agreed. "We'll make sure of it. But we need to hit the can on the first try. And I know about those rifle shoots. She was up against the best down there in Texas."

Billy had troubled thoughts about his new friends being in danger, but he was driven by an inner rage he could not quell.

Inside later that day and after the noon meal, Eloise and Jocelyn were seated at a table with Nellie, busily peeling and coring apples.

There was no sign of Potts.

At a nearby table within their hearing, Red, Marks and Billy sat with Rhyker over coffee. Billy could not help but look toward Jocelyn. *If only*, he thought.

Red gave warning."Don't anyone be quick on the trigger. Maybe it'll all blow over."

"Not likely," Marks said. "Callahan is a man who has to win."

"He has some bad hombres working for him," Rhyker said. "Like Hardy."

As a former ranger with years of experience, Marks had to warn. "If we don't turn over the girl when they arrive, he'll camp the night and wait till sunrise when the sun's in our eyes."

Nellie spoke clearly as she cored an apple. "It will rain."

Red laughed. "Not a chance."

"It will rain," Nellie repeated.

Rhyker looked around his table. "If Nellie says it will rain, it will. Besides, we're overdue for another thunderstorm."

"There's not a cloud in the sky," Red commented. "But just in case, maybe we can move the crates to make it easier to avoid the sunrise."

"What about the dynamite?" Billy asked.

"If it rains? Each of 'em is pretty well sealed," Red answered, "but I don't know."

The four men, with Rhyker the only believer in coming rain, went back outside in the afternoon sun. The sky was clear at every horizon. A breeze was rising from the west.

Billy helped re-stack the crates for better protection. It was good to be doing something other than sitting and waiting. He had been hunting and waiting most of his life. Knowing something might soon bring it all to a roaring climax, he could scarcely control his inner trauma.

Back inside the station later that same afternoon, Potts had come out of his room and sat alone at a table, still grumbling. He glared at Eloise, who chose to sit with Jocelyn closer to the front door. Nellie was in the kitchen with the apples. The other men were outside.

Heartsick, Jocelyn felt love for all these people who wanted to protect her. Knowing they could be shot because of her, it was almost too much to bear.

"Don't worry," Eloise said softly, her hand on Jocelyn's.

Potts, fussing, got up and walked over, glaring down at Jocelyn. "Why don't you be a good wife and go back to your husband? If people get killed, you're to blame."

Jocelyn burst into tears. Potts winced and backed away a step.

Eloise stood up, a little taller than him, and glared down at him. "Why don't you just buzz off before I stuff those spectacles up your rear end?"

Startled, suddenly a little frightened of the Texas woman, Potts sputtered and backed further away. He turned and headed for his room, disappearing down the hallway.

"It's all my fault," Jocelyn said through her tears, just as Nellie came out with a pot of coffee and more cups.

Eloise sat down and squeezed her hand. "Hey, you didn't kill that saloon girl. You didn't shoot your father in the back. Someone has to pay for that, but not you."

"Do not worry," Nellie said, refilling their cups and pouring her own before sitting with them. "Mr. Potts makes trouble, he'll get a lap full of hot coffee."

"I would like to see that," Eloise said with a soft laugh.

"I'm so worried," Jocelyn said.

"For Billy?" Eloise coaxed, trying to distract her.

Jocelyn flushed, dabbed at her eyes.

"I got a feeling that boy is not afraid of anyone," Eloise added.

Nellie sipped her coffee. "Everyone's afraid of something. And that boy is scared silly of you, Jocelyn."

"But he's so hard," Jocelyn said. "So angry inside."

Eloise nodded. "It's a rough country out here, honey. Makes for hard men."

"When Sid was run off, and Billy picked me up in his arms, I fell in love with him." Jocelyn shook her head. "But was it just that he had saved me?"

"No, honey," Eloise said. "Not the way you look at him."

"He is the same," Nellie said. "He looks at you like a sick calf."

Jocelyn flushed with color and stared into her steaming cup of coffee. Her father would have liked Billy, despite the young Texan's obvious drive to achieve some violent goal. If only she had met Billy before Jody had convinced her to marry him.

Eloise, glancing at Jocelyn, thought back to how she fell in love, herself. She wanted to tell Jocelyn to throw caution to the wind. That being with the man you loved made up for any hardships, loss, or pain one must face on the frontier.

Nellie, feeling as Eloise did, said a little silent prayer for Jocelyn.

Later that Friday afternoon, Mintz spoke with Rhyker on the

front porch, while Red, Billy and Marks sat on benches. Mintz held two of Rhyker's Winchester repeaters to go with the weapons he had on the stage. A sack of shells hung from his left arm.

Rhyker looked toward the barn and corrals. "If the shooting starts all of a sudden, take cover and stop them from coming across the road—but just scare 'em, don't hit anyone." Rhyker said. "And come nightfall, all three of you should bunk in the station. They'd like to take hostages."

"I know," Mintz said, leaving the steps and heading for the smithy.

Mintz joined Chauncey and Chipper to work on the stage. They shaped another half circle band of iron. It seemed futile.

"We're gonna run out of options," Chauncey said.

"Nellie wants to get rid of Potts," Mintz said. "She'll have our hides if we don't get it fixed. And worse, she won't give us any apple pie."

Chauncey chuckled. "Yeah, there's no way of getting around her, either."

Later that same afternoon out on the front porch, shaded by the roof from the hot sun, Billy, Red, and Marks were on alert near the rail. They had rifles and ammunition lined up behind the crates, which had been rearranged for better cover and to block the view of the front door.

They could see Mintz, Chauncey and Chipper at the smithy with smoke rising and the coach swaying at every effort.

"You have to hand it to them," Red remarked. "They're bound and determined to get that coach on the road. But Mintz doesn't want my help."

Rhyker came outside on the porch, grumbling. "Potts wants us to give up the girl, and now he's locked himself in his room."

"Let him stay there," Red responded.

Marks adjusted his hat as he stared down the road. "They'll be here soon. I can smell 'em."

Billy's thoughts were spinning. *They are not taking her, no matter what. And I sure want to take a look at that Pike and his left hand.*

In his nightmares, Billy saw the big figure of a man hovering over the well, cussing about his left hand snapped by the windlass and screaming down at Billy. No, he couldn't remember what the man looked like because he was hit from behind, carried face down, and thrown like a sack of wheat into a deep dry well. But if he could face Pike, he could call him on it and get a reaction that might give some answers.

Rhyker stared in all directions at the clear sky. "Sure hope Nellie is right. She says it will come from the west."

"What about their horses?" Red asked. "If the spring is dry."

"I won't stop 'em from using the trough," Rhyker said. "And if they graze 'em north of their camp, at least the horses will be out of the line of fire."

Red nodded. Like the station master, he, too, wanted the animals to be safe.

"I just wish we had the coach ready," Rhyker said.

"No matter," Marks said. "It wouldn't make it past them."

Rhyker looked toward the smithy. "I hope Mintz has a good hold on Chauncey and Chipper, keep them out of trouble. Chipper's too young, and Chauncey won't admit he can't see all that well. But at least they have shotguns."

"Yeah," Red agreed, hands on the rail. "But Chauncey won't even kill a rattlesnake. Just takes a pitch fork and tosses it away. But all they have to do is keep 'em from crossing the road, and I don't think the Callahans will risk being in the open like that."

They paused awhile, staring at the hills beyond the knoll.

"We have time for coffee," Rhyker said at length, staring south at the vacant road.

"I'll wait my turn," Marks replied, as Billy nodded the same.

Rhyker and Red agreed and went inside, leaving Marks, the former ranger, alone with Billy on the porch.

Billy leaned on the porch rail. "They'll probably send Twigs and Jody one more time to make their case before the gang shows up."

Marks nodded. "They won't do any killing 'less they have to. Too many witnesses. So they'll try to scare heck out of us." Marks tugged at his hat brim, stared down the road. "But we have to let them be the first to fire. Once they lay down a barrage, we can blow the top off that thing. But if the lady misses, I figure you can take over."

"She won't miss," Billy said with a grin. "She's a Texan."

Marks leaned back on a crate. "You said you were here to kill some men. Is it Callahans you're after?"

Billy shrugged. "They're a good bet."

"But you're not sure."

"Not yet." Billy gripped the rail and stared south. "Down in West Texas about fifteen years ago, my folks moved us from Kansas to my grandpa's ranch just before he died. Wasn't long before night riders came to murder and burn us out. I was the only survivor."

Marks waited in silence for Billy to continue.

"I was only ten, but I think I hit some of them with a shotgun, right before some big galoot threw me down a dry well. When he fought with the old windless, the handle spun and mashed his left hand, and I heard how Pike Callahan has a crooked left hand."

"Not enough proof, Billy."

"But if I call 'im on it, I may find out."

"I'll back you up," Marks assured him, "if you do it fair and square."

Billy thanked him with a nod and stared down the road. He had liked Marks even before they met. It was legend in Texas that as a ranger, Marks could be trusted to keep his word, had never shot anyone who didn't fire first, and was the best tracker around. He also said words over the graves of men he had been forced to kill.

As for the Callahans, Billy never had a night without hearing his mother's screams in his wild dreams. He would hear them until the night riders paid the price. Like Twigs always said, it wasn't revenge. It was a reckoning. To make things right.

*   *   *   *   *

West of the station just short of a mile away that Friday afternoon, Wiley came down out of the mountains and made camp with a small fire built in a ring of rocks he had gathered. He made himself some coffee and then settled back with his harmonica.

His music had won over his Cheyenne bride, but he had lost her and their son in childbirth. He had grieved with her father, who had accepted Wiley like a son. Unable to live where he had shared his life with her, Wiley had left the mountains to hunt for the railroads building toward and through the Rockies.

It had been years after the loss of her before he had been able to play music again.

Now he sat playing a soft melody. A born scout and tracker, having lived off the land most of his life, he had a sense that never let him down. Maybe he was creaky and had a backache from time to time, but his intent was to live forever. He was actually grateful to Blair Callahan for hiring him as a tracker, because he knew there were other hands on the ranch who had tracking skills. For some reason, he and Blair had connected and forged an unlikely friendship.

Abruptly, Lightning swung his head up from grazing, ears back, and looking past Wiley to some brush a little higher up.

Something stirred high in the mesquite. A varmint? *Yeah,*

Wiley thought and continued playing as he shifted his weight for a better view.

All of a sudden, a blue and white speckled dog of less than medium size was peering out of the mesquite. Wiley kept playing and waiting. The animal, a young female, was covered with burrs and had scratches on her ears. She was thin and ragged.

Now the dog came down the slope and moved closer as it sniffed for food. Wiley reached in his nearby pack, took out a chunk of hard tack, and tossed it near the fire.

The dog wiggled forth and lay down to chomp on the hard bread.

"Hey," Wiley said, lowering his harmonica, "you're one of them Australian fellahs. A blue heeler."

It lifted its head and stopped chewing to listen.

"Yeah, them sheep herders must have left you behind when they was run off. Now if you're anywhere as smart I think you are, we'll get along fine. Hey, you thirsty?"

Wiley dug out another tin cup and dumped water in it from his canteen. He leaned over to set it within reach. The dog shuffled forward and quickly drank from it.

"You're a little bit too skinny there." Wiley's voice was soft and low. "You can stick around. But you got to have a name."

Wiley held out his hand, and the dog came to him as if they were old friends.

"I'll call you Abby, after my ma, God bless her." Wiley said, stroking her neck as she lay at his side. "And when you're being really good, I'll call you Blue Abby."

The white mule came forward to sniff the dog, which wagged her tail before the big animal turned away, having given his approval.

"We'll have to fatten you up," Wiley said to the dog. "And get them burrs off you."

Maybe it was his voice, or maybe it was his soft buckskins, but the dog made herself at home, right next to him. The instant trust the animal had in him brought tears to his eyes. He put his hand on her neck and shoulder, stroking gently.

The sudden howl of a lone coyote echoed in the night.

Abby sat up and growled, then let out a low bark. Wiley petted the dog, calmed her down. He gazed around at the clear sky in all directions but shook his head as he sniffed the air to the west. "You'll get yourself a bath come morning, on account of it's gonna rain."

Maybe being alone was what Wiley had chosen, but not now, not with this homeless dog at his side. Having company was a good thing.

* * * * *

Riding north from Seven Springs later that afternoon, the Callahan gang took a break along side the stage road, breathing their horses and checking their weapons.

Blair concentrated on his mount's bridle while Potluck bent his ear. Hardy and some of the other hands took time for a smoke nearby. The ten hard cases from Cinch kept to themselves and yet not with each other. As tough as Hardy was, he wanted nothing to do with them and made sure he never turned his back to them.

Jody walked over to where Sid stood alone, drinking from a canteen. Jody had not forgotten being turned away from Rhyker's. The embarrassment stung and made him ache for his bride.

"That Billy Tyson looked real mean, but he can't be near as fast as you," Jody said.

Sid drank from his canteen and didn't meet his brother's gaze. "He's a killer, so you can't trust him to be fair in a fight."

Jody fretted, looking for comfort. "My wife could get hurt."

"No, kid, they'll have her someplace safe. You'll get her back, one way or another."

"I never wanted anything more," Jody said. "I know I ain't much on the ranch, and I know I act like a fool at times, but she made me someone special."

Sid was touched, surprising himself. He had never put much store in his kid brother, but he could see the boy had been yearning for someone to make him whole. Finding a bride had given him hope to take his place in the world, and Sid had to feel just a little sorry for him.

Twigs and Hardy walked over to them. Jody, still worried, had questions.

"What do you know about this Billy Tyson?" Jody asked Twigs.

"Not much. But I hear he's the fastest gun in Texas."

"But Sid can take him, right?" Jody asked.

"Yeah, sure," Twigs replied. He knew Sid would probably plug him if he gave away any hint that Sid had been treed and shamed. Neither he nor Sid looked at each other.

Hardy pushed his hat back. "Don't matter, kid. Tyson will go down with the rest of 'em."

"The boss don't want no killing," Twigs said.

"What he wants," Hardy said, "and what he'll get are two different things."

Jody fussed. "How's this getting my wife back?"

Hardy threw in a suggestion. "Maybe the passengers will throw her out."

Sid put his hand on Jody's shoulder. "Don't you worry, Jody. You'll have your wedding night. *And* your honeymoon."

Hardy looked away to hide a snicker. He would have never let the girl out of his sight and would have claimed her even before cutting the cake.

At the same time Jody whined his complaints, Potluck, over by the campfire, was still bothering Blair. "Those fellas from Cinch, they sure look mean."

"I gave 'em orders," Blair said. "No killing unless I say so."

"Why is Rhyker protecting the girl?"

Blair turned from his horse and pushed his hat back. "Nothing else he can do, being the kind of man he is. I'm not sure about the rest of 'em."

Deep in his thoughts, Blair knew he was on a wrong track, but he rose above it.

CHAPTER 6

At the station's smithy late Friday afternoon, Chauncey, Chipper and Mintz continued to work on the stagecoach. Frustrated, they tried different ways to make the undercarriage safe, but luck was not with them. Everything they tried ended up with the coach leaning one way or the other.

"Maybe somebody upstairs doesn't want you to leave," Chauncey told Mintz.

"Tell that to Nellie," the driver said in a grump.

"Not me," Chauncey said with a chuckle. "I'm scared of her."

"You should be," Mintz said with a grin.

Under the shade of the roof on the front porch, Marks and Billy Tyson sat on crates near the front rail. Billy was uptight, ever driven, ever with a single destination—that of justice.

Marks adjusted his hat. "What are you going to do about the girl?"

"What?"

"Get married? Have kids?"

"What?"

"Get a better vocabulary for yourself?"

Billy drew a deep breath, had to grin and finally shrugged.

"She could do a lot better. I have nothing to offer."

"You could get a job with Rhyker. Or Red Linstrom."

"Not a fit."

"Wear a badge?" Marks persisted.

Billy shook his head. "I want what my folks had. A spread of my own."

"And a wife and kids?"

"Yeah," Billy said, "but it may never happen."

"I felt the same once, but I took a chance."

"You're married?" Billy asked, surprised.

"When I met her two years ago, I gave up the badge. She's with our son down in Amarillo with her folks, but I have a ranch near Austin, got a good foreman. And it's time for me to go home."

"And are you going to?"

"I needed money for stock so I took a job with the line, but I miss her, and I won't do her any favors by getting myself shot. I'd hire you on if you wanted. In time, I'd set you up with a starter herd."

Billy could not help but feel blessed. "Maybe, but first…"

"Yeah. First."

They stood watching the road to the south. Billy didn't want Marks to be hurt, and Marks felt the same about Billy. Yet neither of them had planned for a fight with Blair Callahan over a hapless young runaway bride. It was something they could not walk away from, regardless of Billy's quest, for he would be right here in the fight, just the same.

After a moment, Rhyker and Red Linstrom came outside in the late sunlight.

Billy liked these men, all of them, but they were focused on keeping the girl from harm. He agreed with that, but he had already waited too long for his own relief.

They were all silent with their thoughts for a time.

Until they saw riders coming from the south. All four men stood at the rail. Billy swallowed hard, his hands tight on the frame. Marks was to his left. To their right, Red and then Rhyker.

First in view was Blair Callahan, straight in the saddle, riding like he expected everyone to bow in his path. Coming up on either side of him, his two sons. Right behind them, his brother Pike.

"That must be Blair's brother," Red remarked from the porch.

Billy could not see Pike's left hand as the big man rode with the others behind the knoll and into the gully, but he did have a good look at his mean face before he turned west. He had no doubt Pike was capable of throwing a boy down a well.

There were twenty men, including Hardy and Potluck, following the Callahans. It was easy to spot the ten hired guns. They were men who had no regrets, were heavily armed, and looked right dangerous.

From the porch, Billy and his friends watched as all but Jody and Twigs rode out of sight behind the knoll. The two of them headed for the porch. Twigs looked casual as he always did. Jody looked desperate.

Billy only knew one thing. The girl was going to stay.

Jody reined up in front of the porch, as did Twigs, who spoke for them.

"Mr. Callahan asks," Twigs said clearly. "Are you surrendering the girl?"

"No," Rhyker replied.

Jody did not look surprised, just pained. "She's my wife."

"Not anymore," Rhyker said.

Twigs gestured back to the knoll. "They will be making camp for the night. We'll be grazing the horses out on the flats, but Mr. Callahan asks the courtesy of your water trough as needed."

Rhyker nodded. "Yes, if it's just one man at a time and he stays in the open."

"He agrees," Twigs said, having anticipated the response at Blair's direction. "And he says you have until sunup to surrender the girl, so now's as good a time as any."

"No," Rhyker repeated.

"They won't leave without her," Twigs said. "Whatever it takes."

"She stays," Rhyker said.

Twigs looked directly at Billy and then Marks. Slowly, he turned his horse to head for the gully. Jody took a minute longer as he tried to look disdainful, then hurried to follow Twigs to safety.

The men on the porch considered the situation.

"Come sunup," Red remarked, "we don't give 'em the girl, they'll hit us with all they got. And we'll be looking right into the sun."

Rhyker shook his head. "My wife said it'll rain by then."

"She ever been wrong?" Red coaxed.

"Nope."

"But we can't trust 'em," Marks said. "We have to be on our guard all night."

"I'll put Chauncey and Chipper inside by the back door," Rhyker said. "Mintz can take turns out here. Come daylight they can go back to the smithy. But I told 'em to stay out of trouble. All I want 'em to do is not let anyone cross the road."

Red made a face. "They have good cover."

"Old man Callahan doesn't want any trouble with this station," Rhyker said. "Or the line. He'll try to intimidate us before it gets out of hand."

"What's in the crates?" Billy asked.

Rhyker gestured. "Boots, blankets, harnesses. Clothing. They're heavily packed, so don't worry."

Billy stared at the clear sky in all directions. They all had the same thought. Would the sun be in their eyes come sunup, or would clouds and rain give them shade as Nellie predicted?

*   *

Late that Friday evening after supper, Potts had retired to his room. Most of the men were sleeping or taking a turn on the porch.

Jocelyn could not sleep and ended up with Eloise as they helped Nellie make pie crusts in the kitchen.

Even later that night, the smell of hot apple pies in the oven had drifted into the front room where Eloise and Jocelyn sat at a table by themselves. No one else was around. Both women were so sleepy, it wasn't long before Eloise jostled her friend and marched her off to bed.

Chauncey, rifle across his knees, slept in a chair just inside the back door, which had a small, high window on either side. Chipper was asleep in the nearby room which they shared and would take a turn later.

Red and Mintz were in their rooms asleep, and Rhyker in his quarters, waiting their turns on the front porch.

Outside, behind the crates, Billy sat on a bench to the left of the front door, keeping watch while Marks slept on an opposite bench. The night sky glistened with twinkling stars and rising moon. It was cold, penetrating their warm coats, but they also had blankets.

Of a sudden, Marks sat up and yawned in the pale light. He stood and looked around. "Too bad we couldn't have posted Red's border collie out here. Good watch dog."

"Won't leave the wagon," Billy said, standing.

"Yeah, I know," Marks said with a grin. "He's a vicious little guy if you invade his territory."

They gazed toward the knoll, behind which light and smoke from campfires drifted skyward.

They both looked up at the cloudless night sky, but then it was just past midnight. A slight wind was rising and insistent. Both had blankets around their shoulders.

As they stood in silence, Billy thought of Jocelyn. If only he didn't have this mission of revenge. If only he had more to offer her. Marks had made him an offer of a job. Would that support a wife and family? How would he ever earn enough for a place of his own?

Maybe he could homestead a section of land, somewhere.

He remembered how happy his father and mother had been, but that memory was laced with the horror of their murder. He could still see his mother's yellow hair when she brushed it while sitting on the porch in the morning sun. Sometimes she would sing softly in a sweet voice.

To the east of the station and behind the rocky knoll that same night, several campfires burned in the big gully as the Callahan men spread around nearer to the canyon entrance. Two were up on top of the rise using rocks for cover, one on guard to the north and one to the south. All the others were asleep in their bedrolls. Their horses were hobbled and grazing further north and east of the road.

Potluck, awakened hours before daylight, was first in the camp to notice clouds darkening the sky, but he didn't put much store by it. He relieved a roving guard. His post was to watch in all directions while two other men, recently replaced, watched the station from atop the rise.

Always wanting to curry favor with Blair, Potluck moved around where the boss was sleeping. He stood a moment, then started to turn away.

"Potluck," Blair muttered under his hat.

Potluck stopped, alert. "Yeah, boss?"

"What time is it?"

"I don't know but it'll be sunup in a couple hours."

Blair did not lift his hat. "It's still pretty dark. Walk over to the corrals with a canteen in case they spot you. When you're behind the smithy, see if you can get around to where the wagon sits outside the south barn. If you can get in the wagon, stay there. Be a good place to call the shots. Keep 'em from leaving the station on that side."

Potluck felt very important. "Sure, boss."

Over on the covered front porch hours before daylight, Billy and Marks could see the fast moving clouds coming west from the rocky hills. The rising wind had an icy chill. They could see Potluck up the road in the starlight and fading moon, moving north through the horses. He was carrying a canteen as he crossed the road to the corral water trough.

"Which one is it?" Marks asked under his breath.

"Don't know. Too small for a Callahan. Or that Hardy."

"You see him?"

"Not now."

Potluck disappeared behind the smithy and worked his way into the south barn. He was feeling pretty darn smart right about now. He looped the canteen strap around his neck and shoulder so it would hang untended. When he exited the barn, he saw Wiley riding up behind the station on his white mule. He made a face, hoping Blair would be mad about that. Potluck always figured that Wiley enjoyed too much favor from the boss, and maybe this would make trouble for the old hunter.

Potluck snuck over to Red's wagon where it sat in view of the station with the tongue pointed toward the road. Potluck slipped around to the back of the wagon. He reached the already lowered tailgate. He found a hand hold on the frame.

He felt pretty clever, believing he had not been seen. This

would make Blair proud of him, maybe give him some better job.

As he started to climb onto the tailgate, all heck broke loose.

A ball of black and white fur leaped out on him with a terrifying growl. Potluck gasped, was hit hard and bit on the nose before he fell back and off the tailgate. He landed on his backside with a painful thump and stifled a yell. He rolled back away from the wagon and sat up, staring at the snarling Kip leering down at him from the tailgate.

Terrified the animal was about to jump on him, Potluck struggled to his feet and ran around the barn, through the corrals and past the gate. He headed straight for home, his nose bleeding, not caring if he was seen as he hurried across the road north of the smithy for the cover of the mostly sleeping horses.

Billy and Marks, on the front porch, rose high enough to see Potluck running like crazy in the pale light. They grinned, grateful for a little humor.

However, Potluck was not, and when he slipped back around through the Callahan horses, he accidentally bumped a mule's rump and angrily punched it aside. Whereupon, as he passed the annoyed animal's rear, it suddenly kicked with its hind legs. Potluck went sailing with a gasp and landed on his belly in the stubby grass. Furious, he sat up and drew his weapon, about to blast the mule. Then he thought better of it. Also, his nose was bleeding.

He tried his best to sneak back into camp where someone was already making coffee, even though it was a long wait for sunup. He reached his blankets and knelt to wash his face with water from his canteen.

West of the station and some distance on the prairie behind in the dark, Wiley also saw the clouds from his camp. More important, he was mighty hungry and needed something better than jerky for his new pup, which now was burr free and well brushed.

Two hours before sunup, about the time Potluck was nursing his nose bite, Wiley reined up behind the station with Abby in front of him on the saddle. He could smell apple pie, the aroma drifting out the back kitchen window, which was large and stood open, maybe to cool the pies. No light was seen inside. With a powerful hunger, he urged his mule forward.

He assumed the back door to the small porch, over to his right, had to be guarded from inside. He rode over to the kitchen window and against the back wall. With one hand on the wall and the pup under his other arm, Wiley stood on his saddle. His mule stood perfectly still. The window sill was as low as Wiley's waist.

It was easy to put Abby inside, but now he had to follow. His mule stood quiet and waiting. The smell of the pie was overwhelming.

Inside the kitchen at that same moment, Nellie sat half asleep in a chair, just inside the door to the front room. The lamp on the wall was turned low, making it near dark. Twelve pies were lined up on a table next to the wall opposite her. Her intention was to guard the open window until the smoke cleared and the pies were safe. Then she could close it and maybe sleep before daylight.

The door to the front room was shut. Coffee steamed on the iron range.

It wasn't long before she was alerted by a scratching noise and the cold nose of a pup on her hand. When she sat up straight and saw Abby, she just smiled, because she also saw Wiley's floppy, wide brimmed hat with a feather in the band coming inside the window.

She picked up a wooden mallet, got to her feet and inched forward.

Wiley was half inside now, hands groping for something to hang onto, but finally just touching the floor and careening inside, heels over head. He plopped down as silent as he could but then he clanged against the stove. The pup came over to nose him on the face.

"Okay, Abby," he whispered. "Just be quiet while I fill my belly."

He had just gotten to one knee when the lamp was turned up, flooding the room with light.

Startled, he looked up at Nellie with the mallet. She tried to look vicious.

"Wiley, you crazy old goat. Get up."

He stumbled to his feet and fell back against the window. "Now, Nellie, honey, you know how much I love your apple pie."

"Which side are you on?" she demanded.

"The one with the pies."

Forced to smile, she backed off. "Just sit down."

She closed the window and turned.

He pulled up one of the two chairs. "My mule's outside."

"He can wait." She looked at the dog. "Don't you ever feed that poor thing?"

Nellie found leftover meat with gravy and put it in a bowl for the dog, which ate hungrily. Then she poured them both some hot coffee.

Wiley smacked his lips. "I could smell those pies a mile away."

She dished a large slice onto a plate, took up a fork, and handed it to him.

Hungrily, he dove into the pie.

"Where'd you get the little dog?" she asked.

"The Callahans ran off some sheep herders a few months ago. And this one just came hobbling into my camp last night. I call her Abby, after my mother."

"So tell me again, why were you working for Callahan?"

"Easy work just being a tracker. Good pay."

"And now?" she asked.

"I was bushwhacked by some apple pie. So I guess now I'm on your side."

He looked up with a silly grin.

Nellie sat down, after which the dog leaped onto her lap.

Out on the front porch in the dark, Billy and Marks could smell smoke from the chimney. They knew Nellie did not allow anyone but her husband in the kitchen. They also knew she had baked pies the night before.

Marks gestured. "See if there's any coffee. Maybe some pie."

"You'll get me in trouble. With a rolling pin, maybe."

"She won't hit a nice young fellow like you." Marks said, holding back a grin, knowing Nellie would already be fired up. "Besides, she might have gone back to bed."

"Okay, I'll take a chance, but now you owe me."

Marks finally grinned. "Yeah, okay."

Billy dropped his blanket, drew on some courage, and went inside.

The front room was dimly lit and with no one in sight. The door to the kitchen was closed but light shone underneath.

Billy bravely opened it and entered the kitchen where a lamp was turned up. He stopped in his tracks, seeing an old mountain man downing some apple pie, a little dog that jumped down to greet him, and Nellie.

Abby went right up to Billy, who squatted long enough to be sniffed and to pet the friendly dog. Then he straightened and stood up.

Nellie tried to look mean as she got up and faced him.

"Young man, did you wash your hands?"

Billy looked stricken, unable to answer. She was a bit terrifying.

Wiley grinned. "You must be that big bad gunfighter from Texas."

Billy hesitated. "I'm Billy Tyson."

"And you play the concertina. We have to get together with my mouth harp."

"Sure thing," Billy said, because it was one of the few things in life that he enjoyed, jamming with another musician.

"I'm Wiley."

They shook hands, and Billy couldn't help but stare at the pie.

"I came in for coffee for me and Marks," Billy said. "It's cold on the porch."

"Young man, no one just walks into my kitchen," Nellie said, but Billy looked so chastised, she laughed. "Okay, take a piece for you and Marks."

Wiley quickly took another slice, leaving two in the pan, which she moved to a tin box with no lid. She handed it to Billy with no forks. She put two cups of steaming coffee in with the pie.

Billy stood transfixed, which Wiley enjoyed.

Nellie used the handle to lift the lid on the iron range's firebox. She put another stick of wood inside, stoked it with a short poker until the coals caught the wood on fire, then closed the lid. She moved the pot back over the heat.

"Now remember," she said, waving the stove handle at both of them, "you don't tell anyone you had some pie. I want it to last. And if I come back and there's anymore gone, you'll both be cut off for good."

Billy tried to hold back a grin. He picked up the tin box with the pie and coffee.

Suddenly, they stopped to listen. The sound of rain pounding the roof. The wind beginning to rattle the shingles and windows. One heck of a storm had just hit.

"I was right," Nellie said, looking up.

"So was I," Wiley cut in. "But now I got to tend to my mule."

Nellie gestured. "I'll let you out the back door."

113

"Be sure I can get back in the same way without getting shot."

She shooed both men out of the kitchen, turning the lamp down and closing the door behind her as she followed them. No one was in the front room.

Billy, gripping the tin box with pie and steaming coffee, worked his way through to the front door and outside.

Wiley, the dog at his heels, and Nellie went into the hallway. They could see Chauncey snoring away in the chair in front of the back entrance. Nellie went over to kick him on the boot. Startled, he leaped up, kicked air and went over backwards with a loud flop. And then the little dog was licking his face.

At that moment, Rhyker came out of his quarters. Red popped out of his room down the hall. Eloise poked her head out further down.

And all listened as rain pounded the roof and the wind whistled.

Hurrying outside, Wiley nearly fell on the back steps when Abby charged between his legs. "Gees," Wiley said, "I guess you don't wanna be left behind."

He picked the dog up, and it licked his face. He found his mule dutifully by the wall. He quickly put the pup in front of him on the saddle and mounted. He turned into the rain and headed for the south barn in the dark.

On the front porch just before sunup, rain on the roof, Billy and Marks backed up to the benches to enjoy the pie and coffee.

There were no more lightning strikes. Just heavy rain.

"You think the Good Lord is trying to tell the Callahans something?" Marks mused.

"Maybe so."

"You know," Marks said, gesturing, "they're in that big gully, right at the face of that canyon. It's cut into those hills that go up pretty high further back."

Billy nodded. "Are you thinking what I'm thinking?"

Marks nodded with a grin.

Over behind the gully before sunup, men were scrambling to don slickers and keep the fires going. The rain was heavy, insistent. The sky was dark and threatening.

Blair Callahan looked fit to be tied and growled under his breath as he yanked on his own yellow slicker, rain pouring off his hat brim, and glared up at the storm clouds. He appeared to be certain he could stop this assault with a nasty look, and strangely enough, the rain lightened suddenly to a drizzle.

Men were setting up tarps, expecting more heavy rain.

Potluck knelt by one of the fires, nursing his sore nose and painful behind. Hardy stood nearby under a tarp, enjoying the sight of everyone scrambling.

Sid and Jody helped each other with slickers. Pike already had his on, and the two on guard on the rise had rain gear handed up to them.

It was now daybreak, but the sun was not shining on the station. It was covered by fast moving black clouds and occasional sprinkles of rain. Coffee was brewing on a nearby fire, and they moved closer to it.

Hardy looked at Potluck's red nose. "What happened to you?"

"I fell down." Potluck said. "I was on a scout for the boss."

"Yeah?"

Blair got to his feet and limped over to them as Potluck continued.

"And I saw Wiley riding up behind the station."

Blair grunted. "That old fool."

"He'll go down with the rest of 'em," Sid remarked.

"No," Blair said. "He was just hungry. Leave him be."

Blair turned and walked away.

His sons, Potluck and Hardy, never understood why Blair protected the old tracker, but he had always seen Wiley as a replica of his own beloved father, the only man now living that he admired.

Potluck turned and knelt, trying to stoke the fire. Two men were setting up other tarps by the cottonwoods at the mouth of the canyon, making way for the Callahans to be further sheltered but worried about a return of lightning strikes.

The rain remained a light drizzle from a threatening sky full of dark clouds.

Sid, wearing his slicker, walked over to the tarp under which his father and Pike were alone by a struggling campfire. Coffee steamed on the coals. Flames whipped in the wind.

"These trees aren't safe for us," Sid told them.

"Lightning's stopped," Blair grunted. "Storm's moving west."

"We could make a run for the barn," Sid suggested.

"And look like a bunch of fools?" Blair snapped.

"What if the weather turns really bad?" Sid grumbled.

"It doesn't dare," his father replied with a wave of his hand.

Now there was only an occasional light sprinkle, and clouds were moving fast to the west, but still no sunlight. Blair puffed up, certain his opposition had forced the storm to back off.

Sid knelt to pour some coffee. "The deadline we gave them was sunup."

"You see any sun?" his father snapped.

Sid clammed up and so did Pike. Sid handed his father a cup.

They knew the sun would not be in the station defenders's eyes. No one wanted to say that to Blair. Even when silent, Blair could be terrifying.

Eventually, Blair spoke. "When it lets up, we'll give 'em one more chance."

Sid almost said it was a sign of weakness, but stopped himself in time.

*   *

Inside the station at daybreak, Potts, Eloise and Jocelyn came into the front room where Rhyker and his wife were serving coffee, along with a breakfast of eggs and bacon.

Outside, it was cloudy but only with a light sprinkle. It seemed the worst of the storm had moved away.

Red, Mintz and Chauncey came in from the hallway and sat near the front door, while Chipper remained on guard at the back entrance.

Potts sat alone near the hallway where he could make a fast run for his room if there was trouble. Eloise and Jocelyn joined the other men.

"I'll relieve Billy and Marks," Red said, downing his coffee and standing.

"I'll go with you," Mintz replied, getting up and also drinking down his coffee.

Rhyker gestured. "I figure a couple hours before the rain passes, and by then, the sun will be high up and on the roof."

"No," Nellie said. "There will be hail."

"How do you know?" Mintz questioned.

Nellie ignored him and returned to the kitchen.

"Did I make her mad?" Mintz whispered to Rhyker.

With a grin, Rhyker shook his head. "Nothing rattles Nellie."

Jocelyn looked from one to the other. "I don't want anyone hurt."

"Honey," Rhyker responded to her, "it's out of your hands."

Jocelyn flushed with appreciation. No, she didn't want anyone hurt, but she was also terrified of going back with the men who had murdered her father and a husband who had killed a saloon woman. They'd never let her have a chance to run away again.

Nellie returned with more coffee.

117

Chauncey downed his cup and turned to her. "Every time that kitchen door opens, I can smell that apple pie."

"Not till supper," she said.

"But if there's a fight, we may not be here for supper."

"Then it won't matter," she countered. "Now finish up and go relieve Chipper so he can have breakfast."

No one fooled with Nellie, so Chauncey did as she asked.

Billy and Marks came in from the porch, looking for coffee. Billy ended up sitting next to Jocelyn. She smiled at him in a way that made him crumble inside.

Please don't die on me, Billy, she thought painfully. She found herself dwelling on it so much, she had tears in her eyes.

Visualizing a horrible fight, she got up hurriedly and headed for the hallway to return to her room.

Eloise stood up. "I'd better see to her."

With the women gone, Rhyker looked directly at Billy. "That girl's in love with you, son."

Billy's face went pink, then red. He concentrated on his coffee, holding the cup in both hands. Marks grinned at him, thinking of their earlier conversation.

Outside with daybreak in drizzling rain under a cloudy sky, Wiley now had his mule in the south barn, unsaddled. He curried the animal, watered and found grain for him. Abby suddenly chased a varmint into a pile of wood and iron bars. Wiley wore his slicker and took his Sharps as he walked behind the barn where he could see the corrals. Now he returned to the south door and moved into the drizzle. He could still taste the apple pie.

He looked over to the knoll where Blair was camped. They would be wet and cold.

"To heck with that," he growled and picked up the pup and his Sharps, then headed lickety split for the back door.

*   *

Inside the station's back door, Chauncey let Wiley enter from the wet. Wiley hung his slicker on a wall hook, rested his Sharps in a corner, and picked up his pup under one arm. When he entered the front room, he joined Rhyker and Marks. Billy had gone back outside to the front porch where Mintz and Red had already taken position.

Nellie came out of the kitchen with more coffee and a cup for Wiley. "You're dripping water on my floor."

Wiley grinned because he knew that under her nasty approach was a woman any man would treasure. She reminded him of his Cheyenne wife, who had died in his arms.

Marks looked toward the kitchen. "Every time you open that door, I smell apple pie."

"Just you never mind," Nellie said.

Just then there was a loud roll of thunder that shook the building and rattled the windows.

"Now it will hail," Nellie added and turned back to the kitchen.

On the front porch, Billy, Mintz and Red watched the knoll. Clouds were moving west but were still dark, heavy with possible downpour.

Of a sudden, another loud roll of thunder shook the porch, the station, the out buildings and the camped Callahans.

Billy went to the rail where he could see men's hats on the crest of the knoll.

"Only a matter of time," Mintz said.

"I don't see a safe place for our sharpshooter," Red remarked.

He and Mintz re-stacked smaller crates on top of the larger ones to the left of the front door. They made a tunnel for Eloise's rifle. The stacks were various heights from four to six feet.

119

Drizzle ran off the front and sides of the roof. Out on the flats to the far north, there were occasional flashes of lightning but no strikes close to the station.

CHAPTER 7

The storm continued to move west in the light of morning. Drizzle was just wet enough to keep it miserable. No sun.

In the gully across from the station, the Callahans had little need for tarps and slickers but had trouble keeping fires going with the wet wood they'd collected. The two men on the rocky rise had slickers mainly to protect themselves against the wet ground, unaware that three sticks of dynamite were lined up beneath them.

Another roll of thunder shook their camp and the station.

Blair muttered under his breath as he sat by a flickering fire. He could barely feel the light drizzle as it began to fade. Left over water ran around his boots as it passed through. He glared up at the clouds as if to demand, *whose side are you on?*

Within minutes, the drizzle stopped entirely. Dark clouds remained, but no wet.

Blair stood up and shook the rain from his hat. He acted as if he had stopped the downpour on his own. Puffed up, he strutted around the camp, kicking those still asleep.

His kingly attitude apparently was not welcome up above because, all of a sudden, there was such a loud rumble of thunder across the sky that it was deafening.

As the thunder ended, a sudden torrent of big chunks of hail beat down on the camp. Many were cussing and dodging. Blair hurried to get under one of the tarps.

Over at the smithy, Mintz worked on the stage with Chauncey and Chipper, all staying dry under the roof as the hail beat on the coach.

Inside the station, long after breakfast, Billy sat with Rhyker, Red and Wiley. Marks was stationed on the porch outside.

Nellie brought out a tray with empty cups in one balanced hand and the pot in the other. She then returned to refill the serving pot.

Hearing the thunder and hail as it shook the station left them all silent for a time. The battering of balls of ice was almost tuneful. Wiley's dog huddled between his legs where he sat.

Rhyker leaned back as Billy made ready to go out on the porch. "You and Marks get any sleep last night?"

"We had turns," Billy said.

Rhyker smiled at Eloise, who had returned and sat with them. "What about our sharpshooter?"

"Wide awake," Eloise said.

"How's the girl?" Rhyker asked her.

"Resting. Keeps saying she'll go back before anyone gets hurt."

"She stays," Billy said.

Nellie came out of the kitchen with the scent of apple pie wafting through the doorway. She carried a refilled pot of coffee.

"You know," Red told her, "apple pie tastes good all day long."

Nellie gave him a punishing look. "You can all just wait till after supper."

Billy said thought of the apple pie and how he and Wiley had wiped out a whole one, and that he had shared with Marks. He could still taste the cinnamon. He was also keeping his mouth shut about it.

"They must be getting a real pounding behind that gully," Rhyker said with great satisfaction. "Serves 'em right for coming here like some righteous army."

Red agreed. "Blair Callahan insists on being the big he-bull."

The men were silent for awhile, but Billy worried.

"You think the dynamite's okay?" he asked.

"Yeah," Red replied. "But even if one gets wet, we'll have the others. But let's hope we won't have to use it at all."

"We refuse to deal, they'll lay into us," Rhyker said.

Red nodded. "We got to make sure they don't cross up the road and circle around."

"Mintz knows what to do," Rhyker said. "They'll work on the stage and keep an eye out at the same time. They already have two shotguns and three rifles stashed at the smithy."

Red downed his coffee. "I have to feed my dog. I know he's gonna be pretty mad about the thunder."

"Mad?" Rhyker asked. "I thought it scared dogs real bad."

Red just grinned. "My Kip, he just gets real mad and growls at it."

"Yeah, he's ornery, I'll give you that," Rhyker remarked.

They all noticed Abby hiding under Wiley's chair. "I'll come along," Wiley said to Red. "Maybe the dogs will have some fun."

Billy downed his coffee. "I'll get back on the porch."

"And I could help with the stage if Mintz wasn't so pigheaded," Red added. "I used to work as a wheelwright."

Rhyker looked surprised. "Why didn't you say so before?"

"He knows I did that kind of work, but there was a time I offered to help him with the tree, and he got real testy. Said he knew what he was doing."

Rhyker grinned. "Yeah, I've seen that, but by this time, I think he's ready to listen."

"Give your pup an extra treat," Billy told Red. "One of their men snuck over and tried to get in your wagon during the night. We heard a big howl and off he went running back to camp."

"Good dog," Red happily responded.

"Know which one it was?" Rhyker asked.

"No," Billy said. "Too dark."

Later that morning, Billy remained on the porch to stand guard to relieve Marks, who gladly went inside for coffee.

Billy stood alone at the rail. The weather had calmed with no hail or rain. A breeze was moving the clouds along to the west but there was still no sun breaking through.

He could see two men on the rocky rise, but only their hats.

Red with his dog Kip, Wiley and his dog Abby, and Mintz were out in the smithy, working on the stage. Chauncey and Chipper were back to watering and feeding the horses out in the corrals.

Billy's thoughts spun as he gazed at the knoll.

At that moment, Jocelyn came outside with a blanket around her shoulders. She came to stand with him, but he took her arm and led her back around behind the crates.

"Not safe for you out here."

"I'm just worried."

She sat down on a bench, and he sat near her. She noticed the rifles loaded and stacked behind the crates.

Billy felt uneasy, being so close. Even in her misery, she was still beautiful. He could only think how he had nothing to offer, and perhaps when this was all over, not even his life.

Having had little experience with women, Billy had measured those few by the memory of a mother who had been sweet and kind. Oh, yes, she had paddled his behind when he smarted off, and she had even washed his mouth out with soap. But she had soothed his aches and pains. She had hugged him when he cried over his lost dog. She had sat by him all night when he was sick.

And that fatal night, her screams had left a knife in his heart.

So yes, Jocelyn was sweet and beautiful, and no one was going to harm her ever again. He would give his life to stop it, but he felt that was all he had to give.

"Nothing's your fault," he said, "except being too pretty for your own good."

He felt suddenly awkward and started to rise, but she caught his arm, bringing him back down to the bench. She kept hold of his hand, her own so soft it hurt him.

"Thank you, Billy, for everything."

"You ought to be inside. They could get their hands on you."

"Not with you here," she said.

"I'm just one…"

"More like twenty."

He stared at her expression, that of a woman seeing him as a hero. It was humbling.

He had to change the conversation. "I hear your pa was a good sheriff."

"Yes, he was, and he didn't like Jody."

"But you did."

"Jody was always nice to me. I didn't feel one way or the other about him. I only married him because I was so alone with no family except an aunt back east who didn't want me." She squeezed his hand. "But now you're here."

Billy stood and pulled her to her feet, then released her hand.

"I'll go back inside before I say something foolish," she said with a smile.

"And before I forget you're a married woman."

"I'm not married," she said, blushing. "I mean, not that way." She hugged her blanket around her. "I mean he never…" Now her face was red. "You know what I mean."

Embarrassed, Billy nodded and gestured her to go inside.

She took his arm again, stood on her tiptoes, put one hand behind his shoulder and pulled him down enough to plant a kiss on his lips. A soft gentle kiss. He choked with emotion and could only stare at her as she shyly backed away.

She went to the door, turned to give him a sweet smile, then disappeared inside. Billy, shattered by her impact, went back to the bench and slumped down. That kiss was still on his lips like a rose petal, soft and sweet. *God help me*, he thought.

When Jocelyn came back in to the ongoing breakfast, Marks could see it was now okay to go outside, which he did.

Now on the front porch, it was Billy and Marks. Not even a sprinkle now, but no sunlight had broken through the fast moving clouds as yet. It was approaching midday and no sign from the rocky knoll.

Marks didn't ask about Jocelyn's visit, but Billy had gained a lot of color.

They could see between the barn and the smithy that Chauncey and Chipper were back out at the corrals. They saw Mintz at the smithy with Red and Wiley. The two dogs were dancing around.

Now of a sudden to the east, two men appeared on foot, coming around the south end of the rocky knoll. It was Twigs and Hardy, still out of earshot.

"Let me handle this," Marks said in a low voice.

"I want Twigs with us," Billy whispered.

"Why would he want to be?"

"He's my cousin," Billy answered. "When we moved to my grandfather's ranch in West Texas, his folks followed us from Kansas and opened a store in town. After the night riders burned us out, it was Twigs who found me in the well the next morning. He's been with the Callahans trying to sniff them out."

"And?"

"Twig's folks, they moved back to Kansas."

"And?"

"Like I said, the man who threw me down the well and got his hand smashed, he could be Pike Callahan."

Marks respected Billy's urge for retribution.

At the porch rail, they stood side by side, and now were joined by Rhyker. They watched Twigs and Hardy come a little closer and finally in earshot.

Hardy looked as mean as he was. Twigs pushed his hat back.

"Time's up," Hardy said. "Give us the girl."

"She wants to talk to Twigs before she makes up her mind," Marks said.

"Why him?" Hardy demanded.

"She's afraid of you," Marks said.

Hardy seemed to accept that as a compliment. He sneered at Billy, not believing a kid like that was any match for him.

Twigs went up the stairs and paused with his back to Hardy, taking just a moment to pretend to stumble so he could whisper to Billy. "No Callahans were in the War."

Billy tensed as Twigs went inside. *Not a war injury. Not a dally. Just a spinning handle on a windlass.*

Rhyker escorted Twigs inside and after a few minutes, came back out. He walked over to the rail between Marks and Billy. Already filled in by Twigs, Rhyker knew what to say.

"We're holding Twigs as a hostage," Rhyker told Hardy.

Hardy gave a nasty laugh. "Who wants him back?"

"He stays," Rhyker added.

"And the girl?" Hardy persisted.

"She's not coming out."

There was an awkward moment as Hardy hesitated, then spoke. "Mr. Callahan says you got until twelve o'clock. One hour."

Hardy backed away, his hand on his holster. He hated having to look up at the porch. He gave Billy a leer up and down and then hustled over to the knoll as if he thought he'd be shot in the back. He soon disappeared behind the rocky rise.

Up on the porch, Rhyker pushed his hat back. "Twigs said ten of the men with Callahan are from a place called Cinch."

"That's an outlaw hideout, across the border," Marks said. "If they live through the fight, there may not be anyone left to pay 'em, so maybe they'll back off."

They looked over at the smithy where work on the stage continued. The two dogs were still frolicking and running around. Wiley and Red were telling tales, hands waving up and down.

It also looked as if the coach was now upright, thanks to Red's unsolicited advice.

The work continued but now with promise.

Inside the station, back in the room Eloise shared with Jocelyn, effort by the two women to calm her was working. Nellie and Eloise sat on either side of her.

Wiping her eyes with a handkerchief, Jocelyn shivered.

"I'll get you some coffee," Eloise said and left the room.

Jocelyn sniffed. "Mr. Potts hates me."

"He gets any worse," Nellie said, "I'll salt his food."

"You're really very nice," Jocelyn said with a smile.

"When I'm with people I like."

"How long have you been married to Mr. Rhyker?"

"Five years. I was a widow. No children. A lot of men wanted me. I did not like any of them. Joe was a big blustering nuisance, always hanging around."

"Why did you say yes to him?"

"Oh, he was trading with my brother. I loved him on sight but I didn't let it show." Nellie had a silly look. "When Joe saw me, he wanted me. He brought horses. My brother said not enough. Joe came back with more. My brother said not enough." She giggled. "It went on for a long time. My brother was just having fun with Joe. Finally, he said yes."

"You speak so well. Did you go to missionary school?"

"Yes, when I was little, but then it was Joe. He had a good education and taught me. And how to do numbers. Joe wants children but he said he's too old to make it happen."

"He might be surprised."

Nellie put her hand below her waist. "He will be."

Understanding her meaning, Jocelyn was delighted. "When are you going to tell him?

Nellie giggled. "When it's fun to say it."

Jocelyn put her arm around Nellie and hugged her.

Outside before high noon, the sun was shining at last and directly overhead. Behind the rocky knoll, things were drying out. Blair, always seeing himself as a king, decided to take credit for the storm moving on to the west.

Jody stood at the south side of the knoll, staring at the station. He saw Billy and Marks on the front porch. He could also see men working at the smithy.

Hardy came over to him. "You'll get her back, kid. One way or the other."

"I want to show her I love her, if I get the chance."

"Yeah, you got some unfinished business, all right. Need any advice on that?

"I know what to do."

"Yeah, but you learned with painted ladies. That girl of yours, she's quality."

"What's that mean?"

"No pawing. No grabbing. No pouncing like a bull."

Jody, startled and at a loss, still did not ask for advice.

Hardy grinned and walked back into the camp.

Jody continued to stare at the station. He didn't really know what love was, or what to do about it, but Jocelyn had hair like shining golden wheat... Her eyes seemed to change colors from light to dark blue velvet... She had a smile that set his heart racing... He wanted her for his own.

Sid came over to his kid brother. "Don't worry, they won't make a fight over a girl."

"If they do, she could get hurt."

"No, she'll be safe." Sid looked back to his right at the knoll where two men were on guard near the top. He turned and saw Billy on the porch with Marks and Rhyker, which stung his insides. Known for his unbeatable skill with a fast draw, Sid hated the man who had shamed him. If it was ever known what happened, Sid felt he'd have to leave the territory, at least for a time. Just thinking about it made his face burn and his blood boil.

Sid swore to himself that Billy had to die, one way or another.

"Why did they keep Twigs?" Jody asked.

Sid shrugged. "I don't know, but it's pretty stupid. No one cares about him."

"That Billy Tyson's on the porch. He's scary."

"He'll hang before this is over."

"All I want is my wife."

Sid nodded. Sometimes he felt sorry for Jody, though he did burn with envy when he thought about that beautiful girl belonging to his kid brother. But he also knew that he himself would someday be running the ranch. Jody would just be there.

First, in a short while, a lot of people were going to die.

CHAPTER 8

With the storm having passed and a noon deadline looming, the defenders at the station knew it would not be long before all heck broke loose.

Rhyker had gone out to the smithy where the coach was finally upright and level, with Red's expert help. He advised them to stay safe. Red elected to remain working with Mintz, Chauncey and Chipper.

"Unless you need me," Red said, hesitant.

Rhyker thought a moment. "We're pretty well fortified. And there's still the dynamite. It's also too open for them to rush us, and they can't get by us on our south side. So no, it looks like you're a lot of help with the stage, and it needs to be done. It may take the lot of you—and your shotguns—to keep them from crossing the road."

"Yeah," Red agreed.

"But come nightfall, you need to be safe in the station."

Red turned to Mintz. "Okay with you?"

Mintz shrugged. "Yeah, I guess I don't have a choice."

Rhyker turned away to hide his grin from the driver.

Wiley came forward with his dog. "I'd be more useful helping with the road. Best place for my buffalo gun is at the north barn. I can cover a lot of ground from there. Anyone tries to sneak over, I'll make 'em dance."

Rhyker agreed. "Chipper can go with you and be your runner. He can take care of the stock while he's at it. Just be inside before dark."

"We do that," Wiley said, "and they'll sneak around the barn and get back of the house, so they can surround us."

"You stay out here, it could be worse," Rhyker said.

Wiley knew that Rhyker didn't want Chipper in the line of fire. "Right now I want to say hello to Twigs. See if your lady will give me a snack."

Rhyker grinned and headed back to the station with Wiley and his dog.

To defend the station itself, the line up would be Marks, Billy, Twigs, and Rhyker. Not to mention Potts and the women, including a sharpshooter. They could also easily stop anyone from sneaking across south of the station.

But the dynamite was their biggest weapon.

Inside the station, Twigs was in heaven. Once he said he was Billy's cousin, he was seated alone at a table with Nellie feeding him flapjacks. She refilled his cup and sat down across from him.

Rhyker and Wiley came back inside to sit with them. Abby settled under Wiley's chair. "So you still have your folks?" Rhyker asked of Twigs.

"No, it's just me and Billy now."

They could see that Twigs was devoted to his cousin.

"What do you think they'll do at high noon?" Rhyker asked Twigs. "We have about half an hour to go."

Twigs downed some coffee. "Maybe try to negotiate one more time, I don't know."

"Callahan enjoys a reputation as a man in charge of everything and everyone," Rhyker said. "If he attacks the station because he can't get his son's runaway bride, he won't look so good. Especially having a slip of a girl reject his youngest son. What's more, everyone within a hundred miles counts on our store. Including himself."

"He's not bashful about killing folks," Twigs said without going into detail. "But you're right. He doesn't want to damage the station or kill anyone if he can help it."

"So what's he telling his men?" Rhyker persisted.

"Just that no one gets killed till he says so." Twigs wiped his mouth. "But those boys from Cinch, you can't trust any of them."

"Just eat," Nellie said.

"I like flapjacks," Wiley said as he smacked his lips and held his dog on his lap.

Nellie gave him a half smile and went back to the kitchen.

Twigs beamed with delight. Riding for the brand had been a chore, knowing what he might about West Texas. Being free of them, he just wanted to fill his belly and enjoy the attention. While the getting was good.

Eloise and Jocelyn came from their room to sit with them and share coffee.

"So you're Billy's cousin?" Eloise asked Twigs after being told.

"Yeah, just trying to keep him out of trouble," Twigs said, stuffing himself.

"You have a problem with the Callahans?" Eloise remarked.

"Yeah, from a way back."

Nellie refilled his cup. "More flapjacks?"

Twigs drew a deep breath, figuring if he had room. "Yeah!"

"Anyone else?" she asked, as the women shook their heads.

Wiley leaned forward and repeated. "I like flapjacks!"

Nellie smiled and went back to the kitchen once more.

Jocelyn had so many questions she wanted to ask but just sat quiet.

Eloise spoke for her. "Billy have a girl in Texas?"

Twigs shook his head. "No, he's scared of women. We both are."

After a few minutes, Nellie returned with a stack of flapjacks run with syrup and put them in front of the 'starving' Wiley. He would soon return to the smithy and then to the north barn with Chipper.

Outside on the porch a short time later, Billy and Marks kept watch on the porch, shaded by the roof. Over at the smithy, work was ongoing and the two dogs were still frolicking.

"Won't be long now," Marks said, checking his pocket watch.

Billy felt sweat on his brow and had chills. Fifteen years ago, he had barely escaped the murderers on his grandfather's ranch. For the last ten, he had practiced every day with his pistol. He never missed a shot. He was fast, and because of it, he had never had to kill anyone. There had been great satisfaction in facing down Sid, but nothing was resolved. Not yet.

Behind the knoll in the gully, Pike and Blair sat alone on some rocks with coffee in hand.

The brothers look somewhat alike, but Pike was chunkier and hid his hand often.

"Sid just told me that Billy Tyson mentioned the Bonneville Ranch." Pike grunted. "We know old man Bonneville didn't have any kinfolk."

"No, and he said as much," Blair replied. "The bunch there was just squatters."

"But maybe the squatters had kin."

"Don't matter. Nobody knows who burned 'em out."

"No, they don't." Pike wanted to let it rest.

"It had to be done." Blair leaned forward in the sunlight with secret regret about the raid getting out of hand. "We needed the grass and water. Our wells were fouled by that stinky black oil."

"None of that around here," Pike said, sipping his coffee.

"If I hadn't been shot, I could have saved the woman."

Pike shrugged. "You were shot twice and then got it in the leg. You just keeled over and didn't come awake until it was all over."

Blair had regretted his inaction but also was irked Pike had let it ride.

Pike had other things on his mind. "What do you know about this Tyson, anyway?"

"Came out of nowhere. He's just an upstart." Blair was not about to tell Sid's shameful secret. "Maybe looking to build himself a reputation."

They paused as Potluck came to fill their cups and then left.

"What are you going to do about Wiley crossing over?" Pike asked.

"Nothing. I want him left alone."

"Yeah, I know why. He reminds you of Pa."

Blair shrugged, but he had to nod in silence.

"Except," Pike said, without animosity, "you forget, you were Pa's little pet, and I was the one who got the lickings."

Blair just grinned with memory of being his father's favorite.

Pike gestured. "And what about Twigs? I know you like him, but what if he sides with them at the station?"

"He doesn't count for much."

Pike pushed his hat back. "You really figure they'll fight over a girl?"

"You saw her," Blair said. "What do you think?"

"She's pretty, all right, but she's just a female. Jody's a Callahan, so he'll always be able to get another one easy enough. They know we got money."

"You're saying that's why she married him?"

Pike nodded. "Yeah, it had to be."

Blair made a face, defensive. "Jody's a nice kid."

"Yeah, okay, I didn't mean he wasn't." Pike, thought, *oops*, and hurried to correct himself. "I meant he doesn't know much about good women like her, so he just got lucky."

"He did better with her than you did with your three."

Pike grinned. "Yeah, maybe, but I had a good time of it."

"Didn't the second one have brothers that came after you?"

"Yeah, but she ran off, and I was long gone."

They paused as one of the gunmen from Cinch walked by and over to the foot of the knoll to join the others of his kind.

"Those fellas think they're too good to get up on the rocks on watch," Pike said.

"Yeah, they might get dirty."

Away from his father and uncle, Jody paced near the south end of the knoll. His brother Sid stood nearby, but Sid had worries of his own. Dare he challenge Billy Tyson again? His shame would never leave him if anyone found out what happened the last time. What if Tyson told anyone? What if Twigs shot off his mouth?

Sid started thinking how much he wanted a fight so that Tyson and Twigs both got killed. He didn't care if his brother got his wife back. All he cared about was burying the truth of messing his britches when Tyson beat him to the draw.

Sid also had been thinking about a wife of his own. Not a sweet young thing like Jody's, but one a lot livelier and more fun. He was tired of the food prepared by the old guy out at the cook shed. His father refused to hire anyone except for a once-a-month house cleaning. A wife would cook tasty meals and warm his bed.

Pleased with his thoughts, Sid made plans to go on a hunt for a woman of his choice, just as soon as this was over. He figured no female would refuse to marry a tough guy like him. A rich one, at that. She would, of course, give him a son.

What would Jody's bride give him? Probably a useless little girl.

He made a face as he continued to arrange his future. After he made sure Billy and Twigs were both dead.

Up on the porch in the shade, Marks took out his pocket watch. "Won't be long now."

Nellie brought them coffee and then went back inside.

Billy sat on a bench, and Marks sat beside him. They enjoyed the strong coffee.

"I think Nellie puts ashes in this," Marks said with a grin.

They checked their revolver loads.

They had rifles standing behind the crates. There was a tunnel through the boxes for Eloise to have a safe shot while seated.

"You miss being a ranger?" Billy asked, just to make conversation.

"It was a tough job, but no, I don't fancy doing anymore killing."

"What about today?"

Marks leaned forward, watch still in hand. "Nobody's taking that girl out of here."

Billy agreed in silence, his memory of her kiss dogging him.

They sat deep in thought. A short while later, Rhyker came outside and sat on another bench with a big grin. "Billy, your cousin just keeps on eating. He'll be too stuffed to be much help. Just like Wiley, who'll probably fall asleep out there at the barn."

Billy had to grin in return. Twigs was not only a cousin, but a good friend. And having shared apple pie in secret with Wiley, he now had another friend as well.

"Your lady is a marvelous cook," Marks said. "Sure look forward to some apple pie."

"Nellie's pretty firm on that," Rhyker said. "Nobody gets any until after supper. She says after all that hard work, it just goes too fast."

Everyone assumed Rhyker had secretly already had a slice.

Billy turned away to hide his amusement at memory of his taste of it.

At a half hour to the twelve o'clock deadline, all three stood up behind the crates. Two men were walking from behind the south end of the knoll. It was Pike and Jody.

Billy and Marks went to the rail. Seeing Pike's twisted left hand dangling at his side, Billy could not stop himself and moved to the top of the stairs.

Slowly, step by step, Billy got to the hard ground.

Pike and Jody stopped ten feet away.

"My pa says if you don't give her up by noontime," Jody said, "they'll blow your heads off."

"Step aside," Billy said to Jody.

"You're not listening," Jody snapped, and then hesitated.

Seeing how enraged Billy looked with his eyes blazing, Jody shrunk and moved to Billy's right and kept moving, trying to get clear of him. Now Jody turned and hurried to the south end of the knoll just as his father and Sid came to shoo him out of sight.

Blair and Sid could not hear what Billy was about to say to Pike, nor could the men on the knoll, although Twigs, Marks and Rhyker on the porch were closer and could listen in.

Sid muttered to his father. "What's going on?"

Blair grimaced. "I don't know but Pike can take care of himself," still straining to hear but could not.

Over by the porch, Pike turned to Billy with his back to his brother and nephew and snickered. "You want to die?"

His size and stature had always helped scare off any challenger. In a second's time, he realized this young Texan was not backing off. He saw fire in Billy's gaze, the way his mouth was set. His stance. Pike took a deep breath.

Billy took his time. His throat was dry. "You were at the Bonneville Ranch. Fifteen years ago."

Startled, Pike just sneered. "Why do you care?"

"My family was murdered. And you threw me down a dry well."

Now Pike knew who he was. With the memory of being slammed by the windlass' spinning handle, feeling the constant ache in every movement of his left hand even now, Pike was enraged. Fury rose in his guts.

"You were that squatters' kid?" Pike demanded.

"We inherited that ranch. From our grandfather."

Pike didn't care whose ranch it was. He only knew he had lost any valuable use of his left hand that night. He had suffered for fifteen years. Because of a worthless boy. He snarled at Billy.

"You had that scattergun."

Billy didn't answer but had burning thoughts. *Yeah, somebody hit me from behind, and when I fell, it went off.*

"You shot my brother in the leg."

Pike's anger shifted then from his brother being shot to his crippled left fingers and wrist.

"You broke my hand," Pike growled. "Now I'm going to make you pay."

Up on the porch, Rhyker and Marks stood helpless to stop it, but having heard what was said, neither would have tried.

Twigs, fully aware of it all, held his breath. *Take your time, Billy.*

Billy backed away until there was nearly twenty feet between him and Pike. Billy's eyes narrowed in pent up rage. He burned inside. He let his right hand dangle near his holster. He had waited fifteen years to learn the truth. Now it was time for the reckoning.

He heard again his mother's screams, saw the fire and smoke, the horses running wild, and his father lying dead on the ground. Being dragged to the well, fighting back, then thrown into the depths as he clung to the rope. Hearing the big man's howl of pain. The rope being cut just before he hit the bottom. Falling hard as the rope came tumbling down to cover him.

Now Billy faced the man who had wanted him to die. He tried

to hold back, to take his time, but he was seething with a need for justice.

Pike was a fast draw and unafraid. His own fury was driving him. He was unaware Billy had faced down Sid. For fifteen years Pike had been ashamed of his twisted hand, and obsessed with how he could take revenge.

As the two men stalked each other, Blair and Sid remained at the south end of the knoll, unable to hear the conversation.

They watched Marks, Rhyker and Twigs on the porch. Blair immediately assumed Twigs had turned, but he didn't care right then, because Twigs was just a kid saddle tramp. The only thing that mattered right now was that his brother was facing a gunman who might be faster. His only brother.

Sid put his right hand on his holster. If there was a fight, he could get Billy at the same time and no one would judge him for it. He'd just be protecting his uncle.

"No, son," Blair said. "We want the girl."

Sid grimaced, a little annoyed that Jody came first.

The front door of the station could be seen opening and closing, but they couldn't see Jocelyn making her way behind the crates to follow Eloise, who pulled her down to her knees.

"You should be inside," Eloise whispered, knowing the girl was just sick with worry about Billy. They both huddled next to the stacked rifles and boxes of ammunition. At that moment, Jocelyn was ready to grab a rifle and help Billy, but Eloise held her down.

Still inside, Nellie watched from a window with no sign of Potts.

Out on the porch, Rhyker stood at the rail with Marks, both ready to draw to help Billy if needed, while Twigs held back. They could hear whatever Billy and Pike were saying. They were well aware that Sid and Blair were also holding back while out of earshot.

With a twitch of pain in his left hand as a bitter reminder, Pike's anger drove him to suddenly draw with his right.

Before Pike could clear leather, Billy's Colt was in his hand. Pike froze, not finishing his draw. Losing color, Pike thought he was going to die.

Billy could shoot the man down, but he'd never forgive himself for not being fair, even with his nemesis. Just the same, he had sweat on his brow and his heart was drumming.

Pike, staring at Billy's Colt, knowing he could be shot dead at any second, slowly let his own weapon slide back into the holster and lifted his hand away from it. If reversed, Pike would have finished the job, but now as it was, he counted on Billy being soft enough to do the right thing and let him live.

Watching with his father, Sid had a hunger to draw on Billy, but not face on. He could catch him off guard from here, and if there was a fight, no one could claim he got Billy unfairly. He hoped that Pike would pull a trick on Billy, something, anything.

Blair saw Sid's hand on his holster. "Not now, son."

"What were they talking about? Pike looks really mad."

"No telling."

"I could get him from here, Pa. He wouldn't see it coming."

"Just wait."

Blair had seen Billy's fast draw with amazement, realizing why Sid had lost out. Never had he seen such lightning speed. He had now seen Pike back off, something he had never expected.

Blair had just come close to losing his only brother. He was not about to lose his oldest son. He would be left with Jody, who could never take over the ranch. Blair was becoming a very dangerous man as he raged inside. How dare anyone challenge him or his family? He reigned by fear and had to crush any resistance.

In the bright sunlight, Blair and Sid walked slowly toward the porch but were still a long way behind Pike. Billy watched them, still with his six-gun out and at his side. Hands away from their holsters, the Callahans were aware of Marks, the former ranger, at the porch rail with Rhyker. They were also aware that Twigs was behind them.

"Just don't start anything," Blair muttered to his son.

Blair suddenly halted. He could see his brother hunching a little. He held Sid back.

Billy stood with pistol in hand, watching all three Callahans like an eagle. Twigs started to go down to Billy, but Marks stopped him.

"Billy, get up here!" Marks called.

Billy slowly holstered his weapon. He took another moment. He was about to turn toward the porch when, from the corner of his eye, he saw Pike make his move.

Billy spun aside and drew at the same time. Pike had barely pulled the trigger, missing, when Billy shot him in the upper right chest, high enough for survival. Pike's bullet slammed into the lower porch.

Pike gasped, staggered forward, his right arm suddenly useless as he dropped his six-gun and fell to his knees. He lost color, looked in agony, even though he was likely in shock prior to the expected pain. Worse, he had just been out-gunned by a kid. His pride burned. Now there was blood blooming on his right chest near his shoulder.

Blair and Sid stood ready to move forward from the south, not wanting to trigger any reaction that would further jeopardize Pike's survival. They were still out of earshot. Blair saw that Billy had backed off, but he was ready for anything.

On the porch, Marks, Rhyker and Twigs looked just as ready to interfere. Marks held up his hand toward Sid and Blair, signaling them to back off. Blair respected the former ranger and knew it was not a trick. He ached to help his brother, but he waited.

Kneeling, Pike was in great shock, not sure he would live. Not sure he could use his right arm. He had just been shamed by an upstart, who turned out to be the kid he threw down the well. He was not aware Sid had had a worse experience.

Billy, his weapon still in his hand, moved within a few feet of Pike, keeping near the porch and ignoring the watchful Callahans far back from Pike. He knew Marks, Rhyker and Twigs would cover him.

Pike, eyes glassy, stared up at Billy, who demanded an answer.

"Who killed my father?"

"I don't know."

"Who dragged my mother from the house? You?"

"No," Pike gasped, afraid of being shot again. "That was Hardy and some of the others."

Hardy, Billy thought grimly, *you're a dead man.*

Pike closed his eyes, dazed, then opened them.

"Who else was there?" Billy demanded.

Pike was certain his brother and nephew were waiting to help. He was not about to answer any more questions. He just shook his head, yet frightened of the youth's fury. He recalled his outrage when his hand was smashed, and he still blamed the boy he had tossed in the well. In fact, he hated Billy with an all-consuming passion.

Billy holstered his weapon and edged to the foot of the steps and then moved up to the porch, continuing to watch Pike and the other Callahans, who waited at a distance. Marks then signaled to Blair to approach.

Now, careful and wary, Blair limped slowly forward to help his brother. Sid followed but refused to look up at Billy, who knew why, as did Twigs.

Pike struggled to stay alive and stay upright on his knees. Blair ignored the men on the porch. He could see Pike would be okay, and that his brother would be raging about having Billy beat him to the draw. He moved around his brother and worked to get him to his feet with Sid's assistance.

As Blair and Sid, on either side of Pike, helped him stagger forward, Blair finally glared up at the men on the porch. His fury at Billy was at a boil. He snarled. "I got to tend to my brother, so you got till three o'clock. If she's not on her way off this porch by then, we're going to blast the lot of you."

With the Callahans making their way to the other end of the manned knoll, all was quiet on the porch. Billy joined Rhyker, Twigs and Marks at the rail. They were silent as the enemy disappeared behind the knoll.

They could see Red, Mintz and Chauncey had stopped working on a now upright coach and were looking toward the porch. Wiley and Chipper were out of sight at the north barn.

"I'll go out and fill them in," Rhyker said and took off down the stairs, leaving Marks and Billy at the rail as he headed for the smithy.

"That was quite a draw," Marks said with more than a little admiration.

Billy shrugged his pleasure at the former lawman's comment. He wanted Marks to think highly of him because it filled his need for acceptance.

They didn't know Eloise and Jocelyn were behind the crates until the women got to their feet, startling the men.

"Get down," Marks said quickly.

Jocelyn was pulled back down by Eloise.

"And back inside," Marks added.

The women moved low behind the crates and Jocelyn went inside. Eloise brazenly came into the open and joined the men briefly.

"What was that all about?" Marks asked, nodding to the station door.

"She wanted to help Billy," Eloise said.

Billy flushed and looked away as a smiling Eloise went back inside.

"We got time," Marks said. "You and Twigs go inside and have some coffee."

Billy shook his head and stared at the knoll.

"You're afraid of a slip of a girl?" Twigs asked.

"Yeah."

Twigs grinned. "I'll bring some out."

After Twigs went inside, Marks and Billy were quiet awhile, then Marks sat back on a crate, and after a moment, Billy joined him.

"Now they know who you are," Marks said, gesturing to the knoll.

"And now I know it was them."

"So what's next?"

"Justice."

"With a six-gun?"

"Anyway they play it."

"You know, Billy, hate can take a lot out of a man. Make sure you don't lose yourself."

"There has to be a reckoning."

Marks understood, but he liked Billy and wanted him to live.

While Billy talked with Marks, Rhyker was at the smithy with Chauncey, Mintz and Red.

He told Chauncey to alert Wiley and Chipper at the north barn that plans had been changed and the deadline was now three o'clock.

"We could see the gun fight," Mintz said.

"Turns out Billy and Twigs have a feud going with the Callahans from way back," Rhyker said. "But right now, the deadline has been moved to three o'clock."

"You think the dynamite will end it?" Mintz asked.

Rhyker frowned. "Whatever happens, remember, back to the station before dark."

"They'll cross over if we leave," Red fussed.

"They will anyway, and you'd be all by your lonesome out here." Rhyker looked at the coach. "Hey, it's straight up. Not leaning."

"I hate to say it," Mintz scowled, then grinned, "but Red here is one heck of a carpenter and wheelwright."

Red puffed up a little. "Had to do something to get rid of Potts before Nellie slices him up with her carving knife."

They all grinned, because there was no two ways about Nellie.

CHAPTER 9

With the station on high alert and time getting close to the three o'clock deadline, the Callahan camp waited for Blair's instructions. The men on guard on the rocky knoll were half asleep. The men from Cinch were the most restless.

Behind the knoll in the north end of the gully, Pike was being cared for by his brother and nephew. Only Potluck came to help, always wanting to curry favor, which sometimes annoyed Blair.

Blair finally turned to Potluck. "Keep an eye on the station."

Potluck, feeling important, went to the south end of the knoll.

"Bullet went right through," Blair said, cleaning the wound and fashioning a bandage, then a sling for Pike's right arm.

"So he's a lousy shot," Sid smirked about Billy.

"No," Pete said, hurting as he lay back. "He wanted me alive."

"You mean," Sid snickered, "he could be fast and still aim?"

"Yeah, that's right," Pike admitted.

Sid scrunched his face and looked away.

Only Blair knew Sid had been shamed by the same young gunman. In some ways, Blair secretly admired Billy's skills. Too bad the young Texan was on the wrong side.

Sid and Blair squatted down next to Pike, who was covered with blankets.

Callahan men were on the rocky rise. Cinch gunmen lingered back toward the canyon mouth in the cottonwoods, enjoying a drink and a smoke.

With everyone out of earshot, the Callahans spoke in low voices.

"What are you saying?" Blair asked of Pike.

"He wanted to know about the Bonneville Ranch."

Blair tightened his mouth, still sensitive about the raid that had gotten out of hand.

"Why?" Blair asked, afraid his brother would faint before finishing.

Pike accepted another sip from a canteen held by Sid.

"Pike?" Blair persisted.

"He was the kid with the shotgun."

Blair recoiled in anger. "The one who shot me in the leg?"

"Yeah, and the same one I threw in the well."

Blair didn't remember much after being shot in the leg because he had already been shot and passed out. He didn't even see the boy at the time, but Pike had explained it later. In fact, Pike had told him more than he wanted to know, including what happened to the woman. On any raid, Blair had always had one rule. 'If they fight back, kill them. But leave the women alone.' Shot and unconscious, he had been unable to stop the massacre.

"How the devil did a little kid live through that?" Blair growled. "I know for a fact that well was dry and a good sixty feet deep."

Pike groaned in a twitch of pain. "I had trouble cutting the rope on 'im so he jerked and fell part way, a little at a time, but finally I sent him crashing down. He should have been dead when he hit bottom."

Sid leaned back. He had been on the night raid but spent his time burning the barn and out buildings, setting the stock free and roping corral posts to pull them down. It was only later that he learned about the kid from Pike, but by then, the boy had supposedly died in the well. It made no difference to Sid.

"Get us some coffee," Blair said, and Sid reluctantly rose and went for it.

Pike winced in pain."This would never have happened if it weren't for the girl."

Blair waited until Sid was out of earshot. "Not her fault," Blair said. "So what did you tell Tyson?"

Pike had trouble with his ache but continued. "Nothing about you or Sid, but I let out that Hardy was the one dragging the woman off to the shed. The boy's mother."

Blair pushed his hat back. "Let's not say that to anyone else."

"Maybe Hardy will take the heat off us," Pike murmured.

"He deserves whatever he gets," Blair said of Hardy. "He's an animal."

"Yeah, he can be."

"I only heard her scream." Blair scowled, having been unable to stop what had come next because he had passed out. "I don't know who's got a right to be madder, one of us, or the kid who saw what we did."

Pike, who never saw anyone else's side, was always irritated when Blair got so philosophical, but he tried to ignore it because in the long run, Blair never hesitated to down anyone against the Callahans. The one constant thing was that Blair never wanted a woman harmed. Despite all his faults, Blair had his own brand of chivalry. Maybe he carried a lot of misery from how much agony his wife had suffered for days while dying from childbirth.

Pike tried to shift his weight around. "One thing I know, Tyson's got the devil in him from the look in his eyes. And I hadn't cleared leather when I saw his gun in his hand. I never saw anyone that fast, ever."

Blair put his hand on his brother's left shoulder. "Don't move or you'll start bleeding again. And don't worry about Tyson. We'll take him down some other way."

"If he comes up with proof, we could all end up hanging."

"We could make him out to be a liar, but he won't live that long anyway."

Sid came back with coffee and sat with them. He had not heard their conversation but he could see how tense they were.

Now Hardy came over and squatted. "You doing okay, Pike?"

"Yeah," Pike said. "The kid was a lousy shot."

Hardy thought about it, then got up and walked away.

Pike smirked as did Blair, leaving Sid to wonder why.

Meanwhile, Potluck, near the south end of the knoll, suddenly made a face full of misery. He put his hand on his belly. He never should have eaten so many beans in such a hurry.

He almost doubled up in pain. Frantic, he made his way around the Cinch men and headed up the canyon.

Out of sight of the others, he took down his britches and squatted in the trees.

He began to have trouble and groaned.

There was a sudden, deafening roar from up the canyon. Potluck, startled, thought maybe it was a bear or avalanche or anything but what it turned out to be. When he saw the high water racing toward him, he panicked and grabbed a nearby cottonwood.

The flash flood came hurtling down the canyon, tossing him up and down, tearing off his britches, then picking him up like a feather as he lost hold of the tree, and carrying him toward the camp.

Hearing the roar, Blair and Sid had hurriedly lifted Pike and dragged him out the north end of the gully, knowing the south end was on a slight downgrade.

The Cinch gunmen had had no experience with flash floods and waited too long. They scattered, fell, ran in all directions. Some hurried to climb the back of the knoll.

Potluck came hurtling with the water and debris, landing against the high ground. He clung to rocks, his britches suddenly wrapped across his face by the raging water. The men on guard above were laughing until the water reached them.

Up on the station's front porch, Billy, Twigs and Marks had grins when they heard the rumble, saw water spurting up higher than the rocky top of the knoll. The flood spent itself against it but now hurled southward.

"Not a very big flash flood," Marks said. "But it should tell Blair Callahan that maybe somebody upstairs is a little annoyed with him."

"Better yet," Billy said. "If they hold out till dark, there's going to be a full moon."

The three of them enjoyed the thought.

Over behind the north end of the rise and free of the flood, which was now draining southward, Blair fussed over his brother, then stood up to look at his pocket watch. "They got a half hour."

Sid stood up along side him. "Look, Pa, a wagon's coming."

Blair looked north and saw two farm wagons, one loaded with wooden crates, driven by Tucker, an elderly man with a young boy at his side, and one with piled up hay, driven by Jed Massey and his teenage son. The hay wagon stopped near the north barn to unload.

Tucker continued on toward the station.

"Oh, no," Blair growled, "that's old Dan Tucker."

"He's still alive?" Sid questioned. "Gees, he must be a hundred by now."

151

Blair liked Tucker, had traded with him, traveled to town many times to meet with him, play checkers, tell tales. He respected Tucker and wanted Tucker to respect him. Now it wasn't going to be pleasant.

"He's going to be trouble," Blair said.

Sure enough, when Tucker drove behind the north side of the station to unload the vegetables, eggs, and grain, Rhyker joined him. While Tucker picked up his ordered supplies and some for Massey, he learned from Rhyker what was happening.

Now Tucker came hobbling across the road with a real mad on, and he faced up with Blair, who had stepped out to meet him. Tucker looked older than his ninety-nine years with plenty of wrinkles, weathered skin, thin gray hair, and blazing brown eyes. He wore coveralls with holes in them. His voice was raspy.

"Blair Callahan, have you gone off your rocker?"

"No, but…"

"You better not fire on that station, and it had better be standing when I come around next month. You're not too old for a good whipping."

Blair was speechless. Amused, shaken, ashamed, and awestruck.

"Now we got to get home afore dark," Tucker said. "Massey's wife is about to have her kid. My daughter's with her, but we got to get a move on."

Tucker started to turn, stopped, shook his fist for emphasis. Then he spun and hobbled back across the road where Rhyker met him to close their deal.

Blair stood numb as he watched the old man and boy head out in the wagon, pausing at the north barn to wait for Massey. Soon they were on their way.

Any other man who had said that to Blair would be dead.

Blair worked his mouth. He suddenly felt like screaming. How did he get into this fix? For a moment, he thought he saw soldiers riding across the road. He stared. The soldiers vanished into thin air. Blair felt a chill. He had never worn a uniform, so why were they taunting him?

"Now we're past the deadline," Sid reminded him.

Startled back to reality, Blair turned and signaled to Hardy, who came ready for any chance to use his gun.

"Hardy, we're upping the deadline," Blair said. "Go tell 'em they have until five o'clock to deliver the girl."

Potluck heard. "I'll keep an eye on it, boss."

Blair just nodded, amused. Potluck would not be worth much in a fight.

Hardy, Potluck trailing, walked around the north end of the knoll and back over toward the station.

Blair had an ugly smile on his face as he returned to Pike. Both of the brothers were hoping Hardy would take out Billy Tyson.

Sitting by his brother, Blair's smile faded. He saw soldiers standing in the camp. Uniforms seemed gray. They had rifles at their sides. Blair grew agitated. What the devil? He started to shake, blinked. Now the soldiers were gone.

"Hey," Pike said. "Are you okay?"

"Yeah, sure."

"Don't let old man Tucker get to you."

Blair didn't tell his brother about the visions of soldiers. And, yes, Tucker had surely rattled him.

Over at the front porch, Marks, Twigs and Billy were alone at the time.

"That's Hardy," Twigs muttered. "And Potluck."

Now Hardy was crossing over to them with Potluck stopping just past the knoll where he could not hear what was being said.

All three on the porch had heard Pike say it was Hardy who had dragged Billy's mother to her death. Billy knew his friends were worried, but he now had a chance to clean a big part of the slate. He slowly walked down the steps.

Billy's eyes were like bullets. His mouth was tight.

Hardy stopped some fifteen feet away and addressed all on the porch. "Mr. Callahan says you got until five o'clock to deliver the girl."

"So you're Hardy," Billy said, standing aside from the steps.

Hardy had watched from afar when Billy had out-drawn Pike and had not had a good view of the draw. He fancied himself a lot faster and figured no matter how quick Billy was, he had been a bad shot, nearly missing Pike. Hardy never missed.

"Who wants to know?" Hardy snapped.

Potluck stayed back by the knoll, worried. He didn't notice Blair behind him.

Blair himself was in a quandary. Who was this devil masquerading as a gun hawk? Sent to destroy the Callahans? Blair stayed close to safety, ready to duck behind the knoll. He looked up at the men on top of the rise and signaled them not to interfere. Hardy's death could take the heat off Blair's outfit.

Over by the porch, Billy took a stance, challenging Hardy. "You were on a night raid at the Bonneville Ranch. Fifteen years ago in West Texas."

"So?"

"You dragged my mother out of the house, and you and others attacked her and smothered her to death in the shed."

Saying the words was painful to Billy, but not to Hardy.

"You were there?" Hardy scoffed. "You must have been a little kid."

"Not any longer."

Hardy's face took on a heap of danger. He spread his feet. He sure didn't want this kid repeating something that could get him hanged.

They stood waiting for each other to make a move.

Hardy soon realized he had to draw first, and he did, but before he cleared leather, Billy's six-gun was aimed at him. Hardy paused mid-draw.

This time, Billy only lowered his weapon and pointed it down, inviting Hardy to finish his draw.

Hardy sneered and pulled his six-gun all the way, firing at the same time as Billy.

Billy leaped aside, his shot hitting Hardy in the forehead. Hardy's shot missed Billy and sailed south into space.

For a long moment, Hardy stood dying on his feet in open dismay. Slowly, he backed up, crumpled to the ground and rolled out, staring at the sky.

Billy was not aware that Blair had seen and ducked back behind the knoll.

Potluck, shaking in his boots but never having liked Hardy, inched backward.

"Tell Callahan to come and get his gun hand," Marks called to Potluck. "Before he stinks up the place."

Potluck turned around and shuffled as fast as he could back to the gully.

Billy glared at the dead man, holstered his six-gun, and went back up the porch steps. He was shattered, in great pain but knowing he had just avenged his beautiful mother. It was not the end of it. He moved onto the porch.

"Geez," Twigs said, "Billy, do you know how fast he was?"

Twigs' question just hung in the air.

Marks stood in quiet amazement. Rhyker, having been inside and watching from the window, came out on the porch, wrapped in wonder at Billy's crusade.

Marks pulled his pocket watch. "Not long now."

They saw two men coming over to pick up Hardy.

*   *

As the deadline of five o'clock approached, Blair was grumbling to himself behind the knoll, inside his camp. He felt like a fool, changing deadlines, being dressed down by a friend nearly a hundred years old, seeing his brother shot and surviving Billy's draw, and now having seen Hardy go down.

He limped over to where he could tell Pike, lying against his saddle, and Sid who was standing. They listened in stunned surprise but approved of Hardy's demise.

"Hardy was fast," Sid complained.

"Not fast enough," Pike said. "Nobody can take that kid."

"We'll get him some other way," Blair promised.

Just then Jody came over. "Pa, all this ain't getting my wife back."

For one instance, Blair saw his favored son as the cause of this fiasco, a painful admission. Explosive, at his wit's end, frustrated, Blair snapped.

"Get away from me!" Blair growled, losing his patience, and walked off to the north end of the knoll, just to be by himself where the horses were grazing. He stared at the skyline and was relieved not to see ghosts as he had before.

Jody looked devastated, but Sid came to put his arm around his kid brother's shoulder. "Never mind, Jody. Pa's just having a hard day. Nothing's going as planned."

"Maybe I should try to talk to her again," Jody muttered. "Make things right."

Sid was reaffirming his belief that his little brother had no common sense and was only driven by emotion and what good things he could get out of life.

"Just wait," Sid told him. "Tyson has shot Uncle Pike. And now he's killed Hardy. Pa don't want nobody else going over there."

They paused as Hardy's body was carried into the camp. A brutal, ruthless killer had just died at the hands of an unstoppable gun hawk. The men from Cinch, over in the shade, didn't care.

Over at the station, preparations were under way. Eloise had come out to get down behind the crates on the front porch. She had pulled a bench over to where she would have a clean shot through the tunnel created for her. Jocelyn had followed and sat down beside her.

"I'm to blame for this," Jocelyn murmured.

"Do I have to say it again? Jody killed a saloon girl. Sid shot your father in the back so Jody would not hang. How is that your fault?"

Jocelyn watched Eloise take the repeater lined up for her and work a shell in the chamber. Now Jocelyn did the same with another, knowing now she would do anything to stop anyone from being hurt at the station, but especially Billy.

Rhyker was back inside with his wife. Twigs, Red and Chauncey were putting finishing touches to the coach out at the smithy. Wiley and Chipper were in the north barn.

Marks, Billy and Twigs stood on the porch. Marks checked his watch. They checked their revolvers but also had rifles waiting for them behind the crates. They knew the women were waiting under cover.

"Won't be long now," Marks said.

The three of them took cover behind the crates opposite where the women were.

Marks turned to Eloise, over on his right. "You should aim for the center stick. Maybe they'll all blow."

"No problem," Eloise said.

Now the deadline had arrived.

Behind the knoll, Blair had to stop looking like a fool. The Cinch killers were waiting at the back of the camp, but they could get out of hand. Potluck was at the south end, peering out at the station.

This was it for Blair. He had eight of his own gun hands up on the rocky rise, rifles aimed at the station. He waited another five minutes.

"See the girl?" he called and they signaled no, which fired him up. "I'll give 'em five minutes more."

Blair backed up and stood next to Pike, who was laying against a saddle. Blair squatted by his brother. "I didn't think it would come to this."

"I would have just let 'em keep her."

"Jody's in love with her."

"Yeah, I can see that."

"Now what?"

"I'm going to blast them until I see a white flag."

They saw Jody near the south end of the knoll, with Potluck, but he returned and crawled up the rise to have a look through the rocks among the rifle men.

Blair grimaced. "Jody, get down from there."

Jody acted as if he didn't hear his father. He felt he was being blamed for all of this, but he couldn't help it. He wanted his father's approval, but he longed for his bride.

Blair shouted to the men on the rise. "Hit 'em with all you got and don't give any quarter. Now!"

The sudden roar of rapid gunfire brought a thud of bullets into the crates on the porch, the walls of the station, crackling windows, slamming into the building with a vengeance. It continued for a long while, then stopped at Blair's signal, with gun smoke lingering. The volume of the barrage echoed as if thunder had just rolled.

Blair muttered as he paced. He called up to the men.

"See the girl? A white flag?"

The men signaled no.

*   *

Behind the crates, Rhyker, having slipped outside, squatted down with Twigs, Marks, and Billy. They knew Blair would repeat the attack if they didn't respond. They had to act now.

Rhyker looked over at the women and signaled to Eloise.

Eloise aimed at a stick of dynamite's tin cover in the center of the knoll. She took her time with deadly aim. She fired, her shot echoing, startling the men on the rise.

Now, a deafening explosion as if the world was ending. The other two sticks followed in a frightening upheaval. Complete devastation.

The top half of the knoll blew up in stages like an air borne avalanche. Jody and the eight men flew off like flies. Rocks and dirt filled the air. Others below in the gully were thrown wildly about.

Pike, prone against his saddle, had been hit by flying rocks, one grazing his forehead, but he groggily pushed them aside. Another hit his chest, causing his wound to bleed again.

Blair, tossed like a sack of wheat, landed hard on his back. He panicked because Jody had been up high. The men from the top of the knoll had been killed and lay about in heaps in the gully.

He sat up and saw the dead, and right next to them was Jody, also dead and broken. A frantic Blair got up and hurried over, kneeling by his mangled son. Jody no longer looked like Jody.

Sid came running over to him. "Pa!"

Seeing his brother as his father knelt to caress him, Sid halted.

Blair, shattered, stared at Jody, his eyes wet. He turned to see Pike who looked all right, lying quiet and gazing their way. Sid was right there with his father and was okay. Blair had no idea what he would do next.

With Sid standing by, Blair began to see his wife's lovely face.

He had never accepted her death as long as he had Jody to keep her alive.

"Mary," he said, "look what they did to our boy."

Sid swallowed hard, seeing his father consumed by grief.

"Mary, we have to have another son, because Jody's gone."

Sid got nervous at the way his father was talking and backed away. Potluck came with a blanket to cover Jody.

Blair, losing his vision of Mary, stood up, anger rising in him. "Sid, get those men over here."

Sid signaled to the men from Cinch who had survived the explosion.

Blair wiped tears from his eyes. "Tonight when it's plenty dark," he said to his son and the killers, "around three in the morning, there won't be anyone out at the barn or corrals, so you can circle around. They'll be asleep except for maybe one on the porch, but they won't see you. Sid will be in charge. Just take the station."

"We could burn it," one said.

"No," Blair said. "Just take it and be in charge until I can come in."

"What about the girl?" another asked.

"Leave the women alone."

"Won't be easy to break in," the first Cinch man said.

"The back door will open," Blair said. "I've been through it. A hunting knife will trip the lock through the crack. You can slip in and take 'em by surprise while they're sleeping. Sid's been in there, he knows the layout."

"What if they put up a fight?" Sid asked.

"Then do what you have to do," Blair said, having lost all reason.

Sid silently opposed any action. He thought they should cut their losses. He felt his father had just gone off the deep end. Their mission had failed. Jody was dead. The whole territory would hear how the Callahans had made fools of themselves.

Potluck came up and Blair turned to him. "You trail the others and report back to me."

Now Blair turned away from them to watch Jody being covered with more blankets by Sid. Blair had already lost the siege. He had lost his young son. His brother was wounded but able to go home. He had lost a lot of good men on the rise.

Sid turned to his father. "Pa, this is a bad idea."

"Just take control of the station till I get inside. I'll make a big stink about losing Jody, swear at the girl, and then we'll go home."

"We could go home now," Sid said.

"I want them to remember I'm the boss of this territory."

Sid knew his father was desperate to save face, but also that Blair was now irrational and had lost direction, a man he hardly recognized.

Blair walked back over to Pike to see blood on the side of his head. "Pike?"

"I'm okay."

Blair sat down beside Pike, who fretted because he felt as Sid had, that Blair had lost his senses. Jody's death had clearly devastated him. "Bad idea, Blair. It could all blow up in your face."

"I'm not leaving with my tail between my legs."

"And then?" Pike asked, getting no response. "You know there's free grass up in Montana territory, some places it's as high as a field of wheat. Land just there for the taking."

"Not a bad idea," Blair said, grasping at a way out.

"We can start over," Pike said. "Just you and me."

"And Mary," Blair said. "She'll go with us."

Pike winced. "Blair, you know where she is, don't you?"

"She's back at the ranch."

Blair stood up and turned away. His brother stared after him. No, she was buried in West Texas on the old range.

Blair had lost all control of his reasoning. Visions were flashing before him. Jody. Sid. Pike. His wife. Misery. Struggle. Fights with neighbors. All these years. All for nothing. And the soldiers, where were they now?

Pike watched him, worried. Then Pike felt dazed, putting his hand on his forehead.

Over at the station after an early supper, waiting for nightfall, everyone was inside with shades drawn, except for Chauncey and Chipper taking a turn on the front porch. Eloise and Jocelyn were resting in their rooms. Potts was barricaded in his.

The rest of the men later conferred over coffee and finished leftover apple pie with Nellie serving. No one knew that Jody had died in the blast. They suspected Blair would be up to something before long.

Wiley's blue heeler was under his chair. Mintz had his border collie next to him. The dogs seemed content. Twigs and Billy had a lot on their minds. Red and Rhyker were worried.

"Callahan's not going to leave," Red advised. "He has to save face."

"They'll get around us in the middle of the night," Rhyker said. "Then what?"

"We got to take the fight outside," Marks said.

Billy nodded. "We can stop 'em out there."

"And ambush 'em," Marks agreed.

Mintz downed his coffee. "I'll go with you."

"No," Marks said. "Just me and Billy."

"He's right," Billy said. "We can get up on the tank tower. It has a pretty wide platform. And it's real high."

"I can help," Twigs said.

"You're afraid of heights," Billy reminded him.

"The tower's a good idea," Marks said. "And that ladder is too much for the rest of you old folks to climb."

Rhyker snickered. "I'm up there every time a varmint gets in the tank."

"Not me," Red said. "I got one knee won't bend half the time."

"I admit it," Wiley said. "I'd never make it to the platform."

"We'll take turns on the porch," Rhyker advised of Red and Mintz. "But even with a full moon, we won't see 'em if they cross a long way up the road."

"I think we will from the tower," Marks speculated.

"Chauncey and Chipper can take the back door," Rhyker said. "And we can bar the store room door so they can't get in there."

"I'll watch the pie," Wiley said with a grin, just as his dog climbed up on him.

Now Red's dog tried to jump up on Wiley as well.

"Hey, you trying to steal my Kip?" Red asked.

Wiley grinned. "No, but I think he's in love."

CHAPTER 10

Up on the water tower in bright moonlight, Marks and Billy were cold and wishing they had blankets. They saw nothing until three in the morning. They had not been able to see anyone crossing up the road, but they soon spotted movement behind the smithy in the space between it and the south barn.

The ten Cinch killers were soon inside the barn and at the west side door. Sid, who thought it a really bad idea, and Potluck, keeping himself safe, stayed under cover just inside the door.

Sneaking across the open space from the south barn, the ten killers never thought to look up as they pulled their six-guns and headed for the back of the station. They had moved half way across, too late to head back, when Marks and Billy opened fire from the high platform.

Two killers fell, then three more. They fired back, peppering but not cutting through the heavy planks. Three more fell.

The last two Cinch men ran for the trough to get cover. They were cut down before they could reach it.

Inside the barn, Sid steamed. Potluck cowered.

"My pa's going to have a fit," Sid muttered. "Losing Jody hit him hard. Now this."

"I just want to go home," Potluck whispered.

"All over some girl," Sid added in a low voice.

But, Sid thought, *Billy Tyson was still alive and this could be a chance to even the score.* He pulled his six-gun and moved just to the opening in the doorway. He could see Marks and Billy coming down from the tower with their rifles. He only had his six-gun and wasn't sure of a good shot. He watched as they checked to be sure all the Cinch men were dead.

Marks and Billy, looking around at the fallen and expired Cinch riders, were unaware of Sid and Potluck in the barn.

"We just saved Callahan a lot of money," Marks said. "I've seen some of these men on posters, wanted for murder."

Satisfied, they started back toward the station's rear porch, not knowing Sid was sneaking out behind the big trough and windmill, working his way closer out of sight.

They saw Jocelyn, who had pushed her way outside past Chauncey, kneeling on the back porch, her rifle resting on the rail, just as her father had taught her, and aiming in their direction. Under a bright and full moon, she had a good view. They had to assume she was not aiming at them, but just making sure they were okay.

"Boy, does she love you," Marks said.

Billy dragged his feet, following Marks at a distance.

They didn't see Sid slip around under cover, but Jocelyn did. Suddenly, Sid rose to fire at Billy's back. In that instant, she had no choice.

Jocelyn fired, making Billy and Marks hit the dirt.

It was Sid who was hit, staggering backwards, dropping his rifle, failing to kill Billy before he himself was shot in the chest. Marks and Billy spun to watch Sid drop.

Jocelyn was shaken and drained because she had not only saved

Billy but had just shot the man who had murdered her father. She swayed as Chauncey came out to grab her and take her inside.

Marks and Billy went back to find that Sid was dead, shot through the heart.

"She saved your life," Marks said.

Billy was overwhelmed, speechless. She had hit Sid dead center. What a shot! He knew in his heart how painful it must have been for her.

Marks could see that Billy was overwhelmed.

"Okay, Billy," Marks said, "it's over, and now it's up to you. Both you and that girl have a lot of misery to put behind you. Together, you can do it. Just come back with me to Austin."

Inside the station minutes later, Eloise was comforting Jocelyn in their room. Potts was nowhere in sight. Billy and Marks came inside just as Rhyker, Twigs and Wiley hit the hallway with their rifles. The men all returned to a front table. The two dogs slept near the front door.

"We saw from the back porch that the Cinch killers were all dead," Rhyker said, "so we came back inside, and then the girl went past us and Chauncey to go outside. We thought it was over and she was just looking for Billy. Then we heard her rifle."

"What happened?" Twigs asked.

Before Marks could report, Nellie came out of the kitchen with a fresh pot of coffee and more cups. She was beaming.

"I was at the kitchen window and saw Jocelyn shoot down Sid Calllahan," she said, "to save Billy."

Marks nodded. "Sid had been hiding in the barn. He was going to get Billy in the back."

"Sweet gentle girl like that," Rhyker said, amazed.

"Ole Sid never got over being faced down by Billy and messing his britches," Twigs said with a grin shared by Wiley.

Startled, Rhyker laughed.

"That does it," Wiley said to Billy. "Now you have to marry the girl."

"Yeah," Rhyker said. "She saved your life."

Marks slapped a crestfallen Billy on the back. Twigs looked happy.

Waiting a long while inside the south barn to make sure no one came back out of the house, Potluck was so nervous, he almost wet himself. He then scrambled through the equipment and past the stalls, stumbling to a halt when the white mule, untethered, came out of one with his ears back and teeth bared.

Potluck panicked, ran into the corral, fell down, got up and headed for the back of the smithy. He knew he could be seen in bright moonlight as he crossed the road but figured no one would care about him. He made it to the cover of the horses, then headed back to the gully.

Staggering into the near-empty camp, he collapsed near Pike, who appeared to be asleep. He got up and went over to a wide-awake Blair, who had a fire going with coffee steaming. Blair stood up to face him.

"All the Cinch riders are dead," Potluck gasped. "Tyson and some other fellow were on the water tower. They just picked 'em off like a turkey shoot."

"And my son?" Blair asked.

"He was okay till he tried to shoot Tyson in the back. He's dead, boss."

Blair was furious. "Who did it?"

"The girl."

Startled and dismayed, Blair could not react at first. She was the whole reason for the entire fiasco, and now she was the one to end it. It cut him like a knife.

Blair's eyes were brimming. All the wind was gone out of him. He had lost both his sons. He was shriveling up inside. All were dead, except himself, Pike and Potluck.

Blair sat back down, drained. "Potluck, first light, you get one of the pack mules and go get Sid. They'll help you just to get us to leave. Let 'em bury the men from Cinch. They shot 'em."

Potluck looked at the blanket-covered bodies of the eight men at the foot of the rise.

"They can put them under as well," Blair said. "But we're taking my sons home."

Potluck felt bad for the boss, but he realized he himself was now higher in stature.

His eyes wet, a shattered Blair finally got up and moved over to kneel and shake his brother. "Pike, wake up. They got Sid."

He kept shaking Pike until he realized with horror that his only brother was dead.

Blair staggered to his feet and walked back to the fire.

"He's dead," Blair muttered, crumbling to the ground where he sat down, numb.

Potluck poured coffee from the pot for both of them.

Blair worked his mouth in silent anger. His life was falling apart around him. He now saw visions of his wife, of Jody and Sid, the ranch, his brother, the raids, the fights with neighbors. The trail drive from Texas to New Mexico. Checkers with Tucker. It was all fuzzy. All gone.

"I'm sorry, boss," Potluck said.

"We get home, I'm going to sell out and move the herd to Montana Territory. Just you and me with the hands we got left. And my wife."

Potluck was too afraid to comment, for Blair's wife was buried a long time ago down in Texas. Potluck now had the job of taking care of Blair. He felt very important. Shaky, but important.

"They can have the Cinch horses," Blair added. "They've been re-branded so many times, they're useless to us."

The next morning began early with Potluck, unarmed, leading the pack mule around the station with Red and Mintz watching from the front porch.

Potluck was met out back by Marks, Billy and Rhyker, all well-armed.

The Cinch men were covered with tarps. Sid was under a blanket.

"I come for Sid," Potluck said. "But I'll need help."

"We'll lend a hand," Rhyker replied, waving his hand at the other dead. "What about these killers from Cinch?"

"Mr. Callahan says you shot 'em, you can bury 'em." Potluck gestured over his shoulder. "And you can bury our ranch hands on account of you blew them up."

"So what's Callahan going to do now?" Rhyker persisted.

"He's lost both his sons. His brother just died. We're taking them home."

"Jody's dead?" Rhyker asked, surprised.

"Yeah," Potluck tugged at his hat brim. "All that's left is me and Mr. Callahan."

"All this over a girl," Rhyker remarked.

"That's how it started," Potluck said. "But now Mr. Callahan is all broken up. I don't even know if I can get him on a horse. Or his sons and brother."

"You need help?" Rhyker asked.

"Yeah."

They fell silent as Rhyker and Marks helped put Sid on the pack mule and cover him with a blanket, then secure him in place.

"I'll bring Chipper over," Rhyker said. "He's good and strong."

"I'll come along," Marks said. "Billy?"

169

"No," Billy said, turning away.

"Just don't bother Mr. Callahan," Potluck said. "He went up the canyon and won't come out until you're all gone."

By noon, Potluck and Blair Callahan were headed south, leaving the many-branded horses left by the Cinch riders. Their own were trailing. On pack horses and mules, Pike, Jody and Sid were going home.

Potluck was the only one left to serve Blair, a position he had coveted. It would help that, on the ranch, there were still a dozen hands and a good foreman.

Marks, Red, Rhyker and Chipper had helped with the burials, which took all day. They were exhausted by nightfall.

Nellie served a good supper. Potts sat alone, still grumbling.

"You're leaving tomorrow," Nellie said, taking his plate.

"You're all mad," he grumbled. "Stark raving mad!"

Eloise and Jocelyn, still shaken, were in their room. Eloise came out for more coffee, shook her head at questions, and returned.

Later that night, Billy went out on the porch alone to avoid seeing the girl who had saved his life. He would have protected her with his own, but being saved by a young gentle woman was more than he could handle.

He also needed time to ease back into being himself, if he could remember how. He had finally had his fill of Callahans and was just glad to see Blair, the lone survivor of the clan, heading south. Blair, having lost both his sons and his only brother, was being punished by a stronger power than Billy could muster. Hardy had paid for his sins with his life. Yet Billy had trouble letting go of the past.

Twigs came out on the porch to sit near him on the bench. The moon was rising. They were cousins and friends, understanding each other with what they had shared.

"What'll you do now, Billy?'

"I don't know."

"You can come back to Kansas with me."

"Marks offered me a job on his ranch near Austin. Said he'd help me get a start."

"What about the girl?"

Billy shrugged, shaking his head. He had no answer.

Marks came outside to join them. "Tomorrow is my last run. Will I see you in Texas, Billy?"

Billy liked Marks so much, he nodded. "Yeah, the Marks Ranch, near Austin."

"Anyone can tell you how to find us," Marks said. "And Twigs, want to come on down with Billy?"

"Yeah," Twigs said, delighted. "Maybe I'd better keep an eye on him."

"There's plenty of work for both of you," Marks said, "and just like I promised, Billy, I'll help you get a start with your own spread."

"I'm thinking Twigs and I could go partners," Billy said to Twigs' happy nod.

"We got a cabin near the river," Marks said to Billy. "You can have it, you and your bride. And after a time, it's a good place to give you a start. You and the girl."

Billy was rattled, shaken. "Not me. She could do better."

"Hey," Twigs said, "she's crazy in love with you."

"Yeah," Marks said. "She also saved your life. She owns you now."

Twigs and Marks finally went back inside, knowing Billy needed time, but they ran into Jocelyn as they entered. She had been pushed by Eloise to find Billy.

"Go get him, honey," Marks said as Twigs nodded and grinned.

*   *

Alone on the porch in the bright moonlight, Billy had just caught his breath when Jocelyn came to his side at the rail. She smelled of roses and soap. In a blue checked gingham dress just like his mother had worn. She was too close now.

Skittish, he jumped aside, unable to speak, afraid to look at her.

"Billy," she said, "don't you have something to ask me?"

"What?" he finally stammered, staring in another direction.

"Now that we know I'm free, if you asked me to marry you, I would say yes."

"What?"

"All you have to do is ask."

He turned pale then red, still unable to turn.

"Oh, why wait? I'll just say yes right now and marry you."

"What?"

She reached up, turned him around, pulled his head down, shoved his hat back, and kissed him full on the lips.

Billy felt his legs buckle underneath him. He shivered down to his boots. Unable to stop himself, he put his arms around her and hugged her to him as he kissed her back.

Holy Cow, he thought, *boy, does she taste good.*

Having peered out to watch, the whole gang, except Potts, came out on the porch to cheer. Rhyker turned up the outside lamps. Everyone crowded around the couple. Eloise and Nellie were beaming. Twigs could not stop grinning, nor could Wiley. Red felt he should take credit for getting them together in the first place.

There was much joy, teasing and laughter.

"Something I didn't tell you," Chauncey said to everyone. "Years ago, after the War Between the States, I was so sick over all that death and destruction, I became an ordained minister, but I was so lousy at giving sermons, I just let it ride and went to work for the line, then the station."

Everyone stared at him. Chauncey squared his shoulders. He had always been proud of his being a minister, but he had felt like he wasn't worthy and had put it behind him. Now, he was even thinking of starting a church.

Rhyker grinned at him. "No wonder you won't even kill a bug. I guess even they are one of God's children."

"So you can marry these kids?" Marks asked of Chauncey.

"Sure can."

Billy, lost in love for the first time, could only hug Jocelyn to his side and grin.

"And you can baptize newborns?" Nellie asked Chauncey.

"Yep," Chauncey said.

"Hey, honey," Rhyker said with a chuckle, "give the kids a little time."

"Not theirs," Nellie said. "Yours."

Rhyker stared at her, gasped, sat down on a bench, hand on his chest. "What?"

Nellie came to sit at his side. "Take a deep breath."

"Honey, you mean…?"

"You're going to be a father." She hesitated at adding shock. "It will be twins."

Never finding her wrong in her predictions, it was too much for Rhyker.

He drew a deep breath, stumbled to his feet, turned and grabbed Nellie's hand, lifting her in his arms and swinging her around. They were both laughing.

"Hey, everyone," Eloise cut in. "I'm leaving on the stage tomorrow, so I want to see a wedding before we leave."

Mintz cut in. "Stage won't leave till noon."

"Ten o'clock wedding!" Nellie got free of her husband and

grabbed Jocelyn's hand. "Come on, girl, we're going to fix you up."

"And we have to bake a cake," Eloise said, excited.

The women disappeared inside with the flustered Jocelyn, while Billy was slapped on the back so many times it hurt. Rhyker had his share on the back because he was finally going to be a daddy.

The following morning, the front room was spiffed up for the wedding. Jocelyn appeared in a white dress with lace and a flowing veil, hurriedly fashioned. She had jewels in her hair, which fell on her shoulders, speckled with gold.

She was so beautiful, Billy could hardly stand. Facing a preacher turned out to be the hardest thing he had ever faced. Yet he could visualize his mother's sweet smile of approval, his father's nod and easy grin. He liked to think they were watching their son find a new life.

Rhyker and Red gave her away. Twigs was first best man; Marks, second.

Nellie and Eloise were dual maids of honor.

Even Potts showed up with everyone else, if only for the food and cake.

When Billy kissed the bride, she had tears in her eyes. So did he.

The wedding was followed by a collection of a few hundred dollars for the newlyweds. There followed music and dancing. Wiley played a sweet ballad on his harmonica, to which the dogs howled so much, they were locked in another room.

A grand wedding banquet had been hurriedly fashioned.

There was dancing to Wiley's mouth harp and Chauncey's guitar.

When the stage left at noon, Billy and Twigs were riding point. Jocelyn, Eloise and Potts were inside with Eloise glad for company around the annoying man from Boston.

Marks and Mintz were on the wagon seat.

As Billy and Twigs grinned at each other, Billy could not believe the joy he had now found in his life. He would give thanks forever more. A beautiful and loving bride, a chance at a new life—what more could a man want?

The breeze was light and cool. Billy's horse seemed to know they were going home.

Twigs was also a happy man. The years had taken its toll on everyone. The idea of partnering with Billy and his bride on their own spread was a joyful thought.

Overhead, a turkey buzzard circled for a look at them.

"Too late," Billy laughed as it sailed away.

ABOUT THE AUTHOR

Western novelist and screenwriter **Lee Martin** grew up on cattle ranches in Northern California. Martin began writing in the third grade and, later in life, wrote and sold 43 short stories before turning to novels with 26 now published. Martin is also a prolific writer of screenplays, mostly Westerns.

Martin's recent novels, *The Grant Conspiracy*, *The Last Wild Ride*, and *Fury at Cross Creek*, all received rave reviews from *True West Magazine* and were based on Martin's screenplays, as is *Fast Ride to Boot Hill*. *In Mysterious Ways*, Martin's new modern suspense Western, received great critical acclaim from *Kirkus Reviews* and *Midwest Book Reviews*. *Trail of the Fast Gun* is the first book of seven in The Darringer Brothers series, all of which have been reissued in paperback and ebook by Vaca Mountain Press, along with many of Martin's earlier novels.

Martin left the practice of law to write full-time, primarily concentrating on Western screenplays and novels, and often converting one to the other. Martin's screenplay for *Shadow on the Mesa*, starring Kevin Sorbo, Wes Brown, and Gail O'Grady, was based on Martin's novel of the same title (Five Star Publishing, 2014). The movie was the second-highest-rated and second-most-watched original movie in Hallmark Movie Channel's history when it premiered in 2013. The film also won the prestigious Wrangler Award given by the National Cowboy & Heritage Museum in Oklahoma City for Best Original TV Western Movie.

Several of Martin's screenplays are currently under option by producers. Martin's novel, *The Siege at Rhyker's Station* (Vaca Mountain Press, 2021), was filmed in the mountains of Southern California in November of 2020 and released in December of 2021 as *Last Shoot Out*, screenplay written by Lee Martin, produced and directed by Michael Feifer, and stars Brock Harris, Skylar Witte, Peter Sherayko, Jay Pickett, David Deluise, Michael Welch, Brock Burnett, Caia Coley, Keikilani Grune, Cam Gigandet, and the legendary Bruce Dern. *The Desperate Riders*, filmed in early 2021, will soon be available on DVD, and the novel of *The Desperate Riders* will soon be in print. To learn more, visit Lee Martin Westerns on Facebook.

·